THE ARCANE IDENTITY

ANDREW S. FRENCH

NEONOIR BOOKS

Book three: Lost in America

Book four: Gone to Texas

Book five: The Final Girl

The Detective Jen Flowers series

Book one: The Hashtag Killer

Book two: Serial Killer

Book three: Night Killer

Book four: The Killer Inside Them

Northern Crime Fiction

Where The Bodies Are Buried

The Ophelia Red series

Book one: Ophelia Red

Crime Short Stories

Call Me: An Astrid Snow Short Story

Dark Snow: An Astrid Snow Short Story

Bette Davis Eyes: Detective Flowers Short Story

Go to www.andrewsfrench.com for more information.

1 LIMBO

Alice Arcane. That's my name. I'd lived a life on my own, but now I had my identical twin sister, Cassie, with me. She'd been fighting monsters for the last two years, but the supernatural world was new to me. We'd met Dracula, fought angels, demons, and werewolves, as well as discovering a secret government organisation that had been collecting supernatural creatures for five hundred years.

But the only thing that mattered now was finding our mother, Mary. I'd spent all my life thinking she'd given me up sixteen years ago, only to discover she'd arranged to have Cassie and me secreted away from the hospital and out of the grasp of two warring archangels: Michael, and Lucy Morningstar, the First of the Fallen.

Kai, the Warwitch of Whitby, had helped us on our quest so far, and now we needed a demon's help to get to Hell and rescue our mother from the Devil.

I smiled at my sister, but she didn't seem too pleased with things. She pointed at the glove in Kai's hand.

'Are you this demon's tailor?'

Kai was already heading towards a large door at the

end of the Impossible Palace and ignoring Cassie's question. I shrugged when my sister looked at me, and we ran after Kai as she exited. The Warwitch was nowhere around as we stepped into the sunlight until we heard a voice calling our names from the graveyard. When we got there, Kai was kneeling in front of a gravestone. I peered over her shoulder at the tombstone, the inscription having faded away.

'The trapped demon needed to be visible where others of its kind could see it. Chains dipped in holy water and the blood of the virtuous bind it.'

The sun caressed my cheeks. 'But where is the creature?'

Kai slipped the glove on to her right hand. 'There were originally two of these, but one is lost to antiquity. They were created to wipe away the veil between this world and...'

She paused as if unsure whether to say the words aloud.

'And where?' Cassie said.

The Warwitch continued. 'The glove reveals the gate between our world and Limbo. And one of you will need to step through it if you want to speak to Bartos.'

'Limbo?' A puzzled frown crossed Cassie's face, her eyebrows appearing to form one long scrunched piece of hair.

Kai wiped the dust from her gloved hand. 'Limbo is the boundary between Earth and Hell, where the dead go to await the decision on their final destination. Before you find Bartos, you may see some unpleasant things, so think carefully if you want to do this.'

'I'll go.' Cassie didn't hesitate and stepped forward.

I grabbed her arm. 'No, Cassie, we'll do this together.'

She shook her head. 'One of us needs to stay here in

case something goes wrong so we can still rescue our mother.'

She was right, but I didn't like it. And I wouldn't have it.

'We both go, or neither of us does.' I was stubborn and determined in equal measure. She must have recognised the futility of arguing with me from the fixed glare I gave her.

'Okay, Alice. Nothing will force us apart again.'

We turned to Kai as she moved the glove over the front of the grave, rubbing at it as if trying to clean away centuries of dirt and weather damage. The grey of the stone changed into a fine shimmering mist.

'I need to close this again while you're in there because there's no telling what might try to come through from Limbo. Set the alarm on your phones for one hour. That's when I'll reopen it.' We did as she said. 'When you get to the other side, you must find a similar gravestone where the demon will be chained. It shouldn't be too far from this point. Bartos will be secured there.'

Cassie put her hand on the top of the gravestone. 'How will we make the demon tell us where the entrance to Hell is?'

It was a good question and I hadn't considered the answer in our rush to find this Bartos. So I could only think of one thing.

'We'll make him a promise.'

'What promise?' Kai said.

I shielded the sun from my eyes. 'To let him keep living.' Then I put my arm into the mist. It was both cold and hot at the same time. It was uncomfortable, but I stepped through all the same. Cassie followed me, a knife in her hand.

I took mine out. 'Perhaps we should think of getting some guns.'

She laughed. 'Get guns in Britain? We'd be locked up as

soon as someone saw us. No. Only a fool relies on something which needs reloading.'

Our entrance was gone, the cemetery and Kai having vanished behind us. We stood on a flat piece of land that appeared to go on into infinity. There was nothing there but a glistening mist, above us only a pale imitation of the sky. I stared at the dust below our feet, seeing an indentation in the ground. I pointed my blade at it.

'There's the chain Kai mentioned.' The mist was still around us, but fading away.

'Let's speak to this demon, then.'

Cassie bent and grabbed the chain. We followed the metal for about a minute as the air cleared in front of us. The silence lay heavily on my head as I glanced in every direction, seeing nothing but the chain and the tombstone it led to.

When we reached it, it was empty.

'This isn't good,' I said.

'Crap.' Cassie scratched her knife on the stone. 'How are we supposed to find him in here? This land looks endless.'

I scanned the area and saw nothing but us. It was a grey desert with mist swirling around in pockets of air. I turned to Cassie.

'What do you know about Limbo?'

'Isn't it a place of the dead?'

'Something like that. It's supposedly a temporary place between entering Heaven or Hell. Like Kai mentioned, it's believed to exist on the farthest edge of Hell, so I guess if this is a holding place between the realms, the other edge of Limbo could be next to Heaven.'

Cassie considered the idea. 'Perhaps we could enter Hell by walking through here.'

I gazed into the endless horizon. 'I thought the same, but we don't know how big this place is. It could take forever.'

'It's bigger than you could ever imagine.' The voice was like splintered rocks brushed against glass. Cassie and I jumped together, blades out in front and pointing at the thing moving towards us. 'This isn't some board game you children have stumbled into, and those pitiful weapons won't help you here.'

I grasped at my throat at the sight of it: a round creature shaped like a giant football pushing through the haze. Resting on top of its spherical torso was a misshapen head straight from a Hieronymus Bosch painting, all of its features out of place and in constant motion. It moved on six spidery legs, which scuttled forward. Fear sped through my veins, but I stopped it from affecting my face, standing unblinking and defiant at this thing from a terrible, twisted nightmare.

Cassie stepped in front of me. 'Come any further and we'll see how pitiful this knife is against that gut of yours.'

The creature belched out a vast guttural laugh which hurt my ears.

'I mean you no harm. My name is Alan and I'm here to offer my services to you as a guide to Limbo.'

Cassie burst out laughing. 'How does something as ugly as you get such an unassuming name?'

Alan's eyes were like watery eggs on the wrong parts of its head, swirling around its face before settling down and peering at Cassie.

'The longer the human body stays in Limbo, the more messed up it gets.'

'You're human?' My voice trembled on my lips.

'I was once. God only knows what I am now.'

Cassie cut to the chase. 'Do you know where Bartos the demon is?'

Alan bounced up and down like an agitated child, his spidery legs threatening to snap under the exertion.

'Oh yes, the whole of Limbo knows where King Bartos and his acolytes are.'

The mist was heavier in the air as I peered at him.

'What do you mean by his acolytes and calling him a king?'

'There should be no demons in Limbo because this is no place for them. It is a realm for those who have not been damned to Hell, but have not earned entrance into Heaven. But then the humans started sending demons into Limbo. Once one of them got free from their chains, they scoured the realm for the rest of their kind. They created an army, and once Bartos had killed the other contenders, he declared himself King of Limbo.'

I stared again at the surrounding desolation. 'Who'd want to rule this place?'

'What choice did they have? They can't return to Hell or the human world unless they find a gateway. Better to reign here than do nothing.' Alan's football-shaped torso spun around and around under his head, and I wanted to throw up.

I pointed my knife towards his continually changing face.

'Can you stop doing that, please?'

His eyes settled into their regular spot and his stomach stopped moving. That's when I noticed he had tiny spindly arms twitching at either side of his bulbous torso.

'Sorry,' he said.

A noise in the distance, sounding like the screech of bats, distracted me.

'What's there to reign over in such a place as this?' The scrambled eggs I'd had for breakfast were disco dancing inside my guts.

Alan rolled around in a circle like a distorted balloon, ready to pop.

'All the souls of humanity not yet in Heaven or Hell are here. Bartos and the other demons have created a prison, and they can feast for all eternity whenever they want.'

The thought of eating anything turned my stomach. Only the increase in noise kept me from spewing my guts over this arid land. The screaming moved closer. Cassie stared into the air while I spoke to Alan.

'Souls are not allowed into Heaven or Hell because Bartos is keeping them here?'

'Isn't that what I just said?' The thing which was Alan's mouth turned inside out and worms wriggled on its tongue. I stopped myself from gagging with a hand over my lips.

'Do you know what that noise is?' Cassie said to Alan. His eyes swirled around again. His tiny twitching fingers pointed at our blades. 'Do you have any other weapons apart from those little knives? Maybe a rocket launcher or a bazooka.'

The screaming was a piercing shriek that shattered the mist. And then we saw them coming straight for us. Harpies, haggard-faced and wild-haired, their teeth bared and spears clutched in their yellowed fingers. I couldn't decide on having my hands over my ears or across my mouth as they dived.

How had it come to this, where I'd gone from worrying about exams and other students to being fearless as howling monsters hurtled towards me?

The harpies threw spears as they plunged at us. I swivelled as one weapon flew by me, its blade glistening past my head. Last week, I'd had a hard time trying to carry a cup of tea and a plate of toast from the kitchen into the living room, but now it was easy to dodge a deadly missile hurled at me from a misty sky. Was this because of what that angel did when he fixed my broken body? Or was it something else?

I grabbed the spear from the ground. The harpy was about to land on me when I shifted my hips. The beast's claws missed me by inches as I thrust the weapon into its face. Its jaw splintered into pieces.

There was no time to rest. Another came straight after it, plunging headfirst towards me. I flicked out my arm and pierced its chest with the tip of the spear. I pushed it up and over my head, finding strength I never knew I had, and threw it into the headstone which once held Bartos the demon. As I turned, Cassie removed her spear from the skull of a harpy. Two more were dead at her feet.

'Look,' Cassie said as she pointed up. More harpies hovered there, gazing down at us through fiery eyes. They hung like that for thirty seconds before flying away and screaming again.

I put my hands over my ears and watched them go, making sure they weren't coming back in a hurry. Then I glanced down at the dead one near me. It had broad wings, razor-sharp talons, a human neck and face, clawed feet, and a swollen feathered belly. Blood seeped from the spot where I'd speared it. I should have felt remorse at killing another living thing, but I didn't.

I stared at my hands and wondered what I was.

'Oh my,' Alan said. 'I knew you wouldn't need those knives.'

I turned to him. 'Where are Bartos and his demon army, and how many of them are there?'

Alan's little hands wiped the sweat from his head.

'He has about thirty followers close to here. Follow me and I'll show you.'

'How can so few control so many?' I said as we walked.

'Demons are the strongest creatures in Limbo, and he commands other beasts such as those things.' His tiny fingers pointed at what we'd killed. The spear was in my hand and I felt like a Valkyrie.

'Take us to Bartos and we'll liberate this place from him.' Cassie said what I was thinking. We only needed to know how to get to Hell, but we wouldn't leave Bartos in charge of those waiting in Limbo. All we had to do was kill the demon once he'd told us what we wanted.

Kill the demon. How quickly I'd turned into a murderer. Alan was jabbering about something as I peered at my hands. Perhaps the killing instinct was always inside me, part of my mother's heritage: Alice Arcane, a Child of the Nephilim.

Alan rolled forward as the mists vanished and light entered from somewhere.

'The weather hasn't been this nice for centuries. Look, you can see the river now.'

He glanced at the great mass of water on our left. Then, he trundled ahead as I edged closer to Cassie.

'How do you feel?'

'I'm fantastic; how about you?' Her eyes sparkled and it was as if I gazed at a better version of myself.

'I'm the same.' I pointed my new spear at the dead creatures fading in the distance behind us. 'You've fought monsters before, Cassie. Was it like this?'

'They were my first harpies, but no, I know what you mean. I've never moved like that before. It was as if I knew where they'd be before they struck. It was the same with handling the spear.' She stretched out her arm and gazed at her fingers. 'It was as if I'd used it all my life.'

I wondered if both of us were changing as I kept a close watch on our surroundings. Apart from the water, which was as grey and empty as the land, there were no living things anywhere. The sky had lost its dark blue and was yellow in hue, though there was nothing recognisable from our world, with no birds or clouds and no smell of anything.

And then it changed.

Cassie pointed towards a great shadow drifting over the water.

'Something is approaching on the river.'

I shouted to Alan. 'Do you know what that is?' We must have been walking for ten minutes since the fight with the harpies.

Alan stopped. 'I don't know.'

His voice trembled with fear, and I couldn't tell if he was lying or confused. His eyes had dropped to either side of his nose. Every time I looked at him, it hurt my head.

Cassie and I strode nearer to the edge separating the land and the water. Shapes twisted beneath the river, shadows which swam and slithered under the liquid. I didn't want to know what they were. I stood back a little in case they leapt out. Then I recognised the significant presence coming closer: it was a ship.

Cassie planted her spear next to me. 'There are people on there.' It was fewer than fifty feet away. 'There are thousands of them.' Her voice shuddered.

She was right. The vessel was wider than it was long, with every space crammed full of desperate humanity. They screamed silently at us, their bodies contorted and exhibiting terror I'd never seen before. Their faces were wide, gaunt and harsh, trembling fingers clutching at sallow cheeks and bulging eyes, pulling out hair and weeping.

'What is this, Alan?' I peered into his strange appearance as he sobbed.

'I don't know. This is something new from King Bartos.'

'Where does the river go?'

The horror ship sailed past us. Some wailing bodies threw themselves over the side, but large nets attached to the craft caught them. As I peered closer, my heart rushed into my throat: the nets were constructed from wide-mouthed rats that bit at the humans in their grasp.

'No one knows. It's too long to travel the length on foot, but some say one end leads to Heaven and the other to Hell.'

'And which way is that ship heading?'

His eyes swirled in circles before oozing below his

mouth, with enough liquid inside them to carry a thousand ships.

'That way leads to Hell.'

The phone beeped in my pocket. Alan jumped as if it was the strangest thing he'd ever encountered. Cassie's beeped as well.

'We've got forty minutes left. If we don't get this done soon, there'll be no time to make it back.' I gazed across the wasteland as the mist returned. 'What's up ahead, Alan?'

His eyes swapped places on his face and he gazed at me.

'You must prepare yourself for what's on the other side. No matter how bad it looks, just ignore it.'

Before I could ask what he meant, our guide stepped through the haze. Screaming filled the space behind us as we followed him.

'Oh my,' Cassie said as we came out on the other side of the fog. Bits of it stuck to my skin, feeling like nothing I'd touched before. It wasn't just wet but alive, wriggling over me before I brushed it off my face and hands in disgust. But, as bad as that was, I knew it wasn't what had stopped my sister in her tracks.

Alan stood a few yards ahead of us, twitching at the front of a row of large trees. They had many branches, all sagging low and swaying in the wind. And the reason they moved so much was they had anguished people hanging from them.

I placed a hand on my cheek. 'What is this?'

Alan wiped a tear from his bulbous eye. 'When King Bartos collects the souls waiting in Limbo to know their fate, he likes to play with them. Some he imprisons on the boat to Hell, others he keeps close by for his amusement. And then there are these poor unfortunates left here to feed his pets.'

'His pets?' Even as I asked the question, I saw the answer coming towards us in the sky.

'Harpies,' Cassie said.

I didn't know if they were part of the same flock that had attacked us before, but they struck with the same vicious intent. The first wave dived with talons outstretched, raking down the bodies hanging from the trees. Then the second group attacked, with huge teeth biting at the heads of the screaming souls unable to escape.

Cassie and I didn't speak, but charged forward together. I'd never been a good runner or particularly fast, but I was now, at least two steps ahead of my sister and reaching the closest harpy before she did. The creature didn't have time to realise what was happening as I thrust the spear deep into its neck. It let go of its victim and howled as the blood spattered out of it. The terrible noise alerted its brethren, who all stopped in their attack and turned towards me. Their look of surprise told me they weren't part of the flock we'd fought earlier.

The two biggest broke away and swooped towards me, with their eyes burning a hateful red. I was ready for them, but wasn't needed. Cassie leapt from behind me like a pole vaulter without the pole, swinging her spear in one large circle and decapitating both harpies in an instant. Their heads dropped at my feet at the same time as my sister did.

She grinned at me. 'I could get used to this.'

The rest of the harpies hesitated before turning to flee back to their master. But I couldn't let them go.

I sprinted forward, grabbed the closest beast by the foot, pulled it out of the air, and threw it to the ground. It snarled at my feet as I pushed the spear up to its neck.

But I didn't kill it.

Alan shook his spindly arms in front of him. 'What are you doing?'

I pushed my face towards the growling harpy below me. 'I'm going to give it one chance to live.'

'Why?' Cassie said.

'Because we have to help as many people as we can while we're here.' I moved closer to the creature. 'Do you want to live?'

Its eyes shrank in fear, and I wondered if it could understand me.

'Yes,' it hissed.

I nodded. 'Good. You've seen what we're capable of. If you do as I say, we'll let you go. If you don't, I'll come back, find you, and send you to Hell via my spear. Do you understand?'

It considered its options for fewer than ten seconds before hissing again.

'Yes. What do you want?'

I removed the spear from its throat. 'I want you to cut down all these people from the trees. Can you do that?'

The beast rose to its trembling legs, with its huge claws cutting into the dirt.

'Yes, I can do that, but King Bartos won't like it.'

Cassie stood at my side. 'It doesn't matter what that demon thinks. He'll be dead long before you release all these people.'

Alan held up his hands and spun around next to me. 'Okay, if you're done here, we need to get a move on. There's one more place to go through before we reach the Kingdom.'

I watched the harpy go about the task I'd set it as we strode past the trees of hanging bodies, telling each one they'd be free soon. Alan's head had stopped twisting on his hips, so I didn't feel like throwing up as I spoke to him.

'What is this place you mentioned?'

He increased his speed and went ahead of us. 'You'll see now.'

Once we'd left the trees, we reached a small hill. Cassie pulled on my arm as we got there.

'What if it's a trap, Alice, and there's an army of monsters waiting for us over the hill? Those harpies could have gone on ahead and warned Bartos about us.'

She was right, but what choice did we have? Plus, I felt as if I could defeat an army all by myself.

'Any army should be wary of us, Cassie, don't you think?'

She laughed as we strode together up the hill and over to the other side. Alan had disappeared, but I forgot about him anyway when I saw what waited for us.

'Bloody hell.' Cassie let go of me.

'No, not quite.' Alan reappeared at our side. 'This is the Limbo of Infants. When I first saw you, I thought that's why two teenage girls were in Limbo, that you'd come searching for the children you'd lost.'

I ignored him and peered at the never-ending sight of babies and small children lying across the land, all of them completely silent.

I clutched at my chest. 'Are they dead?'

He flicked his tiny fingers at me. 'No, no, of course not. The Limbo of Infants is the permanent status of the unbaptised who die in infancy, too young to have committed actual sins, but not freed from original sin. Some of them have been here for so long, they don't know how to cry anymore.'

Anger rippled through Cassie's face. 'Who decides what sin is?'

Alan's eyes trembled like eggs in a frying pan. 'That knowledge is beyond my pay grade. You'll need to speak to God about that.'

My legs gave way and I slumped to the ground, my lungs struggling to work as I peered across the mass of the dispossessed. Cassie sat next to me and took my hand.

'What can we do about this, Alice?'

I squeezed her fingers. 'I don't know.'

Alan puffed out his cheeks, so they resembled giant balloons.

'You can't do anything, girls, but you have to go around them if you want to see King Bartos.'

I resisted the urge to stand and punch him.

'How can we go around them? They go on forever.'

And they did. There was no end to them as I stared across miles and miles of babies and young kids.

Our guide clapped his little hands together. 'No, it's fine. Because you're too old to enter the Limbo of Infants, once you put one foot inside there, you'll step over into the Kingdom. And then you'll meet the King.'

I stood. 'Why haven't these children moved on to Heaven, Alan?'

He scratched at his enormous chin. 'Well, you see, they all should have a long time ago, but King Bartos keeps them here, just like he does with all the other souls, for his amusement and pleasure.'

I gripped the spear. 'So take us to him.' I looked at Cassie. 'It's about time this king met the Arcane sisters.'

And I wouldn't leave this land until he was dead.

3 DEMON'S KISS

I stepped down towards the silent infants, peering at those faces which turned towards me, pleading in their little eyes for help I couldn't give.

Alan was ahead of Cassie and me as I grabbed his tiny arm, hoping it wouldn't come off in my fingers. He stopped twitching and turned as I asked my question.

'What happens if we kill Bartos?'

'If you kill a king, another will replace him.'

I let go of him and turned to Cassie. 'We need to get rid of all the demons in Limbo.'

She shook her head. 'And how will we do that, Alice? Even if we had the time, which we don't since there are only about thirty minutes left for us to get out of here, there must be loads of demons in Limbo.'

My shoulders slumped because I knew she was right. Finding our mother was the priority, but seeing the tortured souls and abandoned infants sent daggers through my heart.

'Okay, we get what we want, but we'll come back one day and remove all the demons from here. Do you agree?'

She nodded. 'Whatever you say, Sister.'

With that, Alan led us over the threshold of the Limbo of Infants, and all the children disappeared. When we stepped forward, a mist separated in front of us, and stretching further than the eye could see was a camp of tents and people. At least. I thought they were people.

Alan skittered to me, his tiny feet bouncing off the ground.

'That is King Bartos's Travelling Kingdom.'

More harpies were in the air, their shrieks and yelps reaching down to us. They moved from side to side, up and down, resembling a murmuration of starlings. Three figures broke off from the camp and headed our way.

Cassie stuck out her neck like a human telescope. 'Those horses are coming here.'

Alan spun around in agitation. 'There are no animals in Limbo. Those aren't horses.'

A thunder of feet bounded in our direction, clumps of dust leaping from the ground as they ran. I gripped my spear, and as they got closer, I knew what Alan meant about them not being horses.

'Oh no,' Cassie said as they pulled up in front of us.

From a distance, they'd looked like horses, but we only saw the full horror of what they were close up. The legs comprised four separate human bodies, squashed and hammered into shape, contorted faces staring out from where the knee would have been on a horse's leg. The torso of the constructed beast was three more people mashed together in some inhuman manner, rolled and beaten into one massive pulp.

Six eyes were dotted around it and stared straight at me, while three mouths bared their teeth and snarled. There was no sign of the noses. The head of the creature was three human skulls moulded into one terrible shape. It was a dreadful sight.

Sitting on these creatures were demons in their pure form, purple-skinned with horned heads. The middle one wore a crown of bones, and I guessed he was Bartos. I fought off the primal urge to flee back into an ordinary, sensible human world and remembered what the demon had done to the people on the boat and the ones hanging from the trees. And burnt into my brain was the image of the Limbo of Infants.

Cassie appeared to handle it better than me. 'Why don't these things collapse under their weight?'

The crowned demon answered her question. 'Humans are much more malleable in this realm, as you'll shortly find out.' His companions laughed as they pulled on the reins of their unholy mounts. 'I am King Bartos, and you've invaded my dominion, slaughtered my harpies, and released my toys hanging from the trees of the dead. You must pay for your crimes.'

I pointed my spear at him. 'You shouldn't be here, demon. If you go now and take the others with you, my sister and I will let you live.'

Bartos glanced at his companions before they all burst out laughing. It was a raucous, irritating sound that set off the harpies hovering above our heads. The sound vibrated all around us and made my head shake.

When they stopped, the King spoke again.

'We cannot leave here, stupid child. You humans imprisoned us in Limbo, so everything we've done here is your responsibility.'

Cassie and I stood together, hands firmly on our spears. We spoke as one:

'We are the Children of the Nephilim and we're here to remove your crown.'

The two lesser demons flinched at our words, but Bartos remained unmoved. I guess you don't become King of anything if bravado easily sways you. He stared straight into my eyes.

'The Nephilim were wiped out centuries ago by God's great flood. You children are liars.'

Time was running out and I had no patience for this.

'Did you send that boat crammed full of people to Hell?' He peered at me as if my question was a trick. So I tried another tack. 'We need you to get us into Hell.'

His laugh was a huge roar bellowing from him. 'Well, child, you could join the next boatload I'll be sending to the Morningstar Army, but you'll have lost your mind by the time you arrive. Those on the boat will suffer for a long time before they reach the gates of Lucy's kingdom.' He pulled at his unholy mount and the creature let out a long, low whine. 'Why do you want to get into Hell?'

'That's our business,' Cassie said. 'Can you help us do it?'

He peered at her. 'You don't want the entrance to Hell from Limbo, so I assume you want to find the entrance to Hell from Earth, yes?'

Cassie stepped close to his mount. 'Can you tell us where it is?'

He contemplated the question, rubbing long nails together on his hands.

'I'll go one better, child. I'll show you where it is.'

I glanced at Cassie. This wasn't what we'd planned, but we were running out of time to get back for Kai opening the door. I checked my phone, seeing fewer than twenty minutes remained.

'Okay, Bartos. But we need to hurry.'

He dismissed my urgency with a wave of the hand. 'Don't worry, child. In Limbo, time is meaningless. Kill these minions and you can use their steeds to get to your destination.'

The other demons glared at their master as he forced his hybrid human-horse creature out of the way. Cassie and I were opposite them.

'What?' I said.

Bartos grinned at me. 'Prove to me you're who you claim to be. If you are, a few demons shouldn't be too difficult for you.'

My sister moved first, pushing the spear into the ground for leverage, then leaping at the demon closer to her. She kicked him from the horror horse as I stood frozen, again, to the spot. Before I could react, the other one thrust his beast at me, mangled bodies rushing across the dirt. I fell and rolled away before those strange human legs trampled me. Dust swirled up from the soil, attacking my face, plunging into my eyes and throat. I coughed it out and wiped my arm over my head. As I regained my sight, Cassie was grappling with her demon as his steed ran around and screamed. Mine turned and charged again.

Bartos ridiculed our efforts. 'If you so-called Children of the Nephilim can't beat two of my lowliest underlings, what good will you be in the forthcoming war between Heaven and Hell?'

I spat dust from my lungs and tried to dodge the legs aiming for my face, succeeding until scrawny human arms uncurled themselves from the beast's leg and scratched at my cheek. They missed my head, but clawed down my arm as they moved past me, tearing shreds from my jacket. The creature turned to come again. In the haze of grime and returning mist, I'd lost sight of Cassie.

My spear had disappeared in the first attack. When the beast rode at me again, I grabbed the demon's leg. I pulled him down and on top of me. We hit the ground together as the fiend let out a terrible scream.

The demon leant over me and glanced at Bartos. 'I'll kill you, child, and then I'll take the crown from that treasonous cur.'

It was enough for me to slip the dagger from my pocket and plunge it into his throat. Yellowish bile and blood flowed from him as I moved to the side and got up. It stank of vinegar and brimstone.

'Are you okay?' Cassie shouted to me. I glanced over to see her pointing the spear at the King on his inhuman mount, one dying demon writhing at her side. I nodded and wiped the blade clean on the beast that had attacked me.

My lungs throbbed and my heart thumped against my ribs.

'We haven't got time to return to the rendezvous.'

We were about to be stranded in Limbo, but all I could think about was killing this so-called King.

'Have you girls ever ridden before?' Bartos turned his mount in the direction we'd come. 'These steeds are fast. They can have you back at my previous prison in an instant.'

What choice did we have? I shivered as I climbed on the creature and took the reins, finding them made from thin strips of flailed human flesh. My skin crawled, but I couldn't let go. This was our only hope. I'd lived with horses for a while, so I knew how to ride.

I turned to Cassie.

'It's easy; you can do it.' She didn't hesitate and

mounted the beast. Alan had disappeared as we followed Bartos to our exit from Limbo.

The creature whined underneath me as we moved forward, jumping into space we'd stepped through from the Limbo of Infants. When we landed, the children were behind us in the distance.

My body ached as I tried to adjust to my ride. There was no saddle, the beast's amalgamated flesh feeling unpleasant against me, and I was glad to be wearing trousers. I glanced over to see Cassie coming to terms with her steed. We rode as fast as a speeding train, and she pulled the beast over to me.

Cassie nodded at Bartos. 'We can't take him with us.'

'I know.' I had a plan.

'What about the souls enslaved here?'

It pained me to think of them all as we approached the now empty trees. At least the harpy had kept its promise, but I knew the people it had released would suffer again soon enough unless we removed all the demons from Limbo.

'We'll return once we've found our mother.'

I promised that to myself and those trapped here. The creature underneath me shrieked again as we reached the stone and the broken chain. The King of Limbo had told the truth and we'd made it there in no time at all. Bartos dismounted and peered at the space where the window to Earth should appear as I glanced at Cassie.

'What century is it on the other side?'

I thought it harmless to tell him. 'It's the twenty-first.'

He picked up the cracked metal which had chained him to the stone so long ago.

'Five hundred years in this place. I'm surprised I haven't gone mad.'

'You'd rather be in Hell?' Cassie dismounted, and I did the same.

He turned to us. 'I'd rather be on Earth, it's much more fun, but even Hell is preferable to the endless bleakness here.' He looked around at the eternal wasteland. 'But I'll tell you where Hell is on one condition.'

Before I could respond, Cassie had her blade at his throat.

'You'll tell us now, or I'll slice your flesh apart.'

'Do that, and it will have been a waste of time you coming here.' His face was expressionless, his purple skin unmoving.

I put my hand on her arm. 'He's right, Cassie.' She grimaced, but stepped back.

He grinned. 'You're such a good pair of girls; you can't be Children of the Nephilim.'

'What's your condition?' I said to him.

He wiped a slither of blood from where Cassie had held the blade.

'You must both promise not to harm me when we return to the other side. If you do that, I'll tell you how to find the entrance to Hell.'

Cassie sighed while I stared at his grinning face and thought of all the tortured souls we'd seen.

It was time to make another deal.

4 TICKET TO RIDE

We found ourselves in the same situation as when we'd confronted Dracula, having to guarantee not to harm something we should kill to prevent human suffering, just to satisfy our selfish needs.

'I promise.' I didn't hesitate, but Cassie was silent. She stared at him, and then at me.

'I promise.' As she spoke, the window appeared. The graveyard flickered on the other side like a television signal settling down into normality, the grass and headstones twinkling into view. The smell returned to the world, smoke drifting through on the breeze from Whitby.

'Are you there, Alice? Cassie?' It was Kai's male voice, anxious and trembling.

The demon looked at me. 'After you, child.'

I marched through, then Cassie, then Bartos. Kai stepped back when he saw the demon.

'Don't worry, Kai; the demon is with us. Close the window now.'

Kai clasped a flaming torch in his hand, even though it was a scorching summer's day. He strode towards the gap into

Limbo with the flame pushed out ahead. Kai lifted the torch up, and then brought it down across the divide, brushing it through the air as if it was a beacon to lost souls. As he finished, smoke fell over the space and settled on the doorway; then, it solidified and returned to the original gravestone with the faded writing.

He turned to me.

'What now, Alice?'

I whispered into his ear. 'Don't worry about the demon. I have a plan. Take us into the Impossible Palace and get me the Blade of Reality.'

Kai faced the former King of Limbo. 'Welcome to my home.'

Bartos looked around the cemetery, staring at the abbey in the distance.

'This looks a lot worse than the first time I was here.' He gazed at the sea. 'To think, those who imprisoned me are long dead and gone, probably to Hell, and their place of worship is reduced to these ruins.'

His apparent joy annoyed me. 'Follow me,' I instructed him. Cassie walked behind as we headed into Kai's invisible home, striding through a gap in the trees as deceptive as it was revealing. There were no complicated stairways this time, no grand monastic hall restored to former glories, only a tranquil dining room with an unlit fireplace guarded by empty suits of armour stationed around the walls. At least, I thought they were empty.

Bartos rubbed his purple hands, long nails scratching against each other.

'What a marvellous construction this is, so cosy and family orientated. Can I live in something like this?' He smiled with enough teeth to fit in four heads.

Cassie glowered at him. 'You're lucky to be alive at all.'

Kai closed the door behind us, and the Blade was in his fingers. Bartos saw this.

'If you instruct your servant to attack me, you'll be breaking your bond, girls.'

I shook my finger at him. 'Stop moaning, you big purple baby. No harm will come to you here if you tell us what we want. Otherwise, my sister will slit your throat, and I'll enjoy watching her do it.'

'No doubt,' the demon said, 'no doubt.'

I removed my phone, checked my messages, and then sent a text. I whispered in Kai's ear as I finished. Cassie glared at Bartos, and then at me. I shouldn't have enjoyed keeping my plan from her, but it was hard not to.

I searched the room for Rufus, disappointed not to find him.

'Now, do what you promised.'

Bartos placed his hands on the back of a sofa. He flexed his muscular arms and body, and I was thankful he was wearing trousers. His grin was of someone who knew something good was about to happen.

'I must admit I haven't been entirely truthful with you.' Cassie and I removed our daggers together. 'But don't panic, Children of the Nephilim. I will help you.'

'Explain.' Cassie pointed her knife at his eyeball.

The former King of Limbo detached his Crown of Bones.

'Understand that most demons are thrust from Hell by the First of the Fallen and given specific instructions. We're not allowed back until we've completed those commands. We demons don't know how to return to Hell; that's something only the Demon Lords know.'

'Who?' I said.

Bartos ran a finger over the bones constructed into royal headgear.

'All the bigwigs, God and the archangels, always have to delegate. So Lucy created Demon Lords to direct her minions while she busied herself with more important things. When the world was less complicated, there were only a dozen of them, but now, there's more than a hundred.'

Cassie inched the blade closer to his face. Bartos never flinched.

'How come I've never heard of them?'

'They rarely interfere with humans. No offence, but you're beneath them.'

'Where would we find a Demon Lord?' I said.

Bartos sniffed the air. 'I assume we're still in Whitby, so that means the closest would be the Demon Lord of the Northeast of England. You'll find them in Newcastle at this time of year.'

My phone vibrated with an incoming text message, so I checked the screen. It was the reply I'd been waiting for.

I returned my attention to him.

'So, that's the information you promised about getting into Hell?'

His eyes sparkled with glee. 'And now you have to keep your promise and set me free.'

'And what will you do here?' I wanted to hear the words from his mouth.

'I'll do what all demons do, just like humans do what they do. We're all creatures of our nature.' He grinned at me. 'Once I find a nice meatsack to wear.' Bartos scratched at his chin. 'I can't decide on male or female this time, or maybe a kid.' His eyes sparkled. 'How I've missed crawling inside those fleshy human frames.' He picked at his teeth.

'They're weak, but demon blood adds a little oomph to that faulty design.'

I resisted the urge to punch his face. This new level of violence simmering in me was disturbing.

'I won't release you here. It needs to be somewhere far away.'

He eyed me with suspicion. 'You promised not to hurt me; both of you did.'

'And we'll keep that promise. I'm sending you away from England, that's all.'

He flexed those impressive arms again and pondered the situation.

'I never liked this wretched country anyway. It's always too cold, and the food is terrible.'

I nodded to Kai. He took the Blade of Reality and sliced a doorway from thin air.

'I'll find you someday, demon.' Cassie scowled not at him, but at me.

'What an amazing object,' Bartos said as Kai peeled away reality.

'You're free to go through there.' I pointed at the gap. Bartos hesitated. Cassie strode forward with her knife. The demon smirked, then stepped into another part of the world.

'Until we meet again, Children of the Nephilim.' He laughed as he disappeared from view.

Kai used the Blade to seal the hole.

Cassie directed all her anger at me. 'Why did you let him go? Where did you send him?'

I showed her the text message I'd received.

I'll welcome him with open arms and a great big smile. Medusa.

'Now, we need a plan of action for Newcastle.' I strode

across the room as Cassie stood there, gobsmacked. I sank on to the sofa and waited for the pictures to arrive on my phone.

Cassie dropped into the seat next to me and laughed. 'How is your new friend?'

'She loves the internet and social media. She's made loads of mates and has even got a date lined up.'

'A date?' Cassie nearly fell over. Rufus appeared from nowhere and jumped into my lap.

'Don't worry. It's in one of those virtual reality games you get online. She's all excited about it.' My phone vibrated as I spoke. I took it out and checked the message. 'And now, she has a nice new statue for the patio.'

Cassie stroked Rufus's head as he purred on my legs. 'Bartos?'

I showed her the photographs on my mobile. The former King of Limbo was frozen in shock, eyes about to burst from their sockets. His arm was outstretched as if to block out the sun. He must have been a fraction too slow.

'I think he makes a nice new addition, though the purple was more vibrant than this grey.'

'I have to admit, Sister, you surprised me.'

Did I detect a hint of admiration in her voice? 'I'm happy to have been of use.'

'Of all the demons I've fought before, he was the first to talk his way out of trouble. And look where it got him.'

I didn't have time to dwell on our success. 'Did you speak to your contact in Newcastle?'

Cassie nodded. 'They'll give us somewhere to stay while we're there.'

'Do they know anything about this Demon Lord?'

'Nope. They've never heard of such a thing.'

And before today, neither had I. God, archangels, Limbo and Demon Lords: it was all new to me.

'And what about the Children of the Nephilim?' What about who we're supposed to be?

Cassie pulled a sceptical face. 'Yeah, I don't know if I believe that.'

I held up my hand and flexed my knuckles. 'Do you feel different?'

Cassie reached out her fingers and intertwined them with mine.

'Yes. I have a sister now. And my mother is out there somewhere, and I know she didn't abandon me; she gave me away to protect me.'

'She protected us both.'

'And that's why we have to rescue her from wherever Lucy or Lucifer or whatever they're calling themselves took her.'

'She's in Hell. I can feel it.'

Cassie hugged me, then we parted. 'We'll find her, Alice. I promise we will.' We peered into each other's eyes. It differed from looking into a mirror: I gazed beyond myself and to the piece I'd been missing all my life.

'I believe it.'

'But you're right, Alice, because I am different. It hit me when we crossed into Limbo, but I thought my senses were out of whack because of that place. I'm stronger, quicker. I can anticipate things like a sixth sense. That's why it was so easy to beat those harpies.'

'I think this is just the beginning, Cassie. Lucy and Michael didn't tell us everything.'

'Do you believe God is returning to Earth to start again, to wipe humanity clean, and only we can stop them?'

I shrugged. 'I don't know what to believe. All I care about is finding our mother and being with you.'

We hugged again, her breathing matching mine, the warmth drifting between us.

'We'll find some demons in Newcastle and beat the truth from them about this Demon Lord.' Cassie let go of me as Kai walked into the room.

'I thought Demon Lords were a myth,' Kai said. 'A former lover told me she'd dated one once, but I didn't believe her considering she also said she was on speaking terms with Elvis, who was alive and well and living in a seaside hut in Redcar.' The Warwitch strode forward and handed me the Blade of Reality.

It was strange in my hand, the metal warmer than I'd expected it to be.

'Are you sure about this?'

'It has to be done. You can't keep rushing back to the windows I'm opening. You only need to miss one for this to be all over. And both of you have proved how resourceful you are. I think I can trust you with this, but don't lose it.'

'Thank you, Kai.' I gave the Warwitch my warmest smile before handing the Blade to Cassie. She seemed surprised.

'You know Newcastle better than me. I'll probably cut a doorway straight into the river.'

She didn't protest and took it from me. 'Okay. I'll get us close to the train station, and from there, we'll head to my contact's place.'

I turned to Kai. 'I'll text you when we arrive.' At my side, Cassie moved the Blade through the air, but nothing happened.

Kai issued instructions. 'Treat it as if you're trying to cut a thin slice of butter. In your mind, imagine where you want to go, somewhere you've been before, so that you can visualise it. Focus on that, and then make a window or doorway with the Blade.'

I watched as Cassie breathed in, then out, her fingers clasped around the Blade. I put my hand on her shoulder.

'Relax and take your time, Sister.'

She did that, moving her fingers through the air, cutting from top to bottom, then across, up once more, finally reaching the point where she'd started. Reality fell away from us, and I peered through to the other side. A train trundled over the tracks nearby.

'We should be outside the station, in the shadows near the wall. It'll look like we've come from the platform.'

Before I said anything, she was through the door and gone. I shook my head at Kai, then followed Cassie through. As I stepped on to the concrete, Kai was already pulling the gap shut. I couldn't see Cassie. There was noise everywhere: people chattering; trains arriving and departing. Someone pulled on my arm, and I reached for my knife as I fell back into the shadows.

'No need for that, Sister; not yet, anyway.' Cassie was next to me, breathing hard.

'What's up?'

'It's harder than I thought, using this thing.' Cassie held the Blade up to my face. 'I cut us into the wrong side. We're inside the station, near the platforms.'

I couldn't understand why she was bothered by that.

'It doesn't matter; it's only a bit further to walk.'

Cassie grinned at me. 'You've never been to a modern train station. We're on the other side of the barriers, and we don't have a ticket to get through.'

She let go of my arm. I leant forward and saw what she meant. Train staff were everywhere, and there was no way out of the station apart from the substantial automatic barriers fifty feet from us.

I wasn't worried. 'Come on, Cassie, we'll charm our way through.'

I'd never charmed my way in or out of anything, but there was always the first time. If I could trick a demon and befriend a gorgon, I must be capable of sweet-talking a rail guard into letting me through without a ticket.

'After you, Alice.'

I strode towards the queue and waited. Cassie was behind me, looking more nervous than when we broke into Dracula's house. I rubbed at my eyes as if I'd been crying. The guard turned to me; he was in his mid-twenties, looking bored and irritated.

'Some bloke snatched the tickets right out of our hands on the train, from my sister and me, and now we're late for the hospital to see our mum, and she's ever so ill.'

His face was a blank sheet of paper.

Cassie fell into him, grabbing his arm and giving it a little squeeze.

'I need the bog desperately, or I'm gonna pee all over the place.'

'I can't let you through without a valid ticket.' His stare was so stony-faced, I thought he'd been on a date with Medusa.

Someone shouted behind us, yelling and hollering like drunks at a party.

Cassie squeezed her legs together and grabbed hold of her stomach.

'I'm gonna have an accident soon, mister.'

Panic consumed his features. He relented and opened the barrier. We were through it quicker than you could say ticket fraud. Cassie clutched my hand and we ran for the exit.

Thick fingers wrenched the smile from my face, pulling me backwards. As I swivelled to see who it was, a group of coppers sped towards us. I stared into the gloomy mug of a serious-looking policewoman.

'Okay, okay. I'll pay for the tickets.'

I reached into my pocket for some money. Before I got there, a massive piece of plastic came crashing down on to my wrist.

I screamed in agony. My knees buckled and I fell to the floor, bringing the copper down with me.

'Officer under assault,' she cried into her radio. I kicked her off me and rolled to the side. I jumped up, looking for Cassie, but couldn't see her. I moved. Then something hard hit me on the back of the neck. The force knocked me into a wall, my shoulder finding fresh pain which spread through my arm.

I grabbed at it with my other hand, staring straight into the grim faces of two coppers, the woman and a bloke who looked like he snacked on steroids for breakfast every morning. They gripped on to batons and blocked my exit into the street. I still couldn't see Cassie.

'You need to come with us, kid,' the man said.

What choice did I have?

I had a fleeting second to think of a way out before the plastic pig flew through the air and hit the male copper in the side of the head. It must have been heavy as he dropped to the floor along with the pig. As his colleague snapped her head to him, I moved, an instinct kicking in I'd never experienced before.

An unknown reflex thrust my leg out and I kicked her below the knee. She screamed as the bone cracked. I was already beyond her when she joined the other copper on the ground. Empty beer cans and sweet wrappers blew around them as I gazed at Cassie six feet away. There were two more unconscious uniformed officers at her feet.

She grabbed my hand. 'Come on. We have to get across the river and find my contact.'

We ran together as the rain came and the adrenalin surged through me.

I grinned at the *Welcome to Newcastle* sign as we headed down to the Tyne.

5 SEASON OF THE WITCH

I wiped the rain from my eyes to see the rats running away from the river's edge. The quayside was close to us and I held Cassie's hand as we ran.

'Why did the police attack us?' I shouted to her.

Cassie let go of me and we stopped, finding shelter in a doorway. She spat water on to the ground.

'I don't know, but we'll be safe once my contact meets us here.'

'Who is this contact?'

She brushed wet hair from her eyes. 'Someone I met in a foster home a few years ago. She knows the supernatural is real.'

I lifted my damp arm and pointed towards the river. 'Is that her near the bridge?'

The rain had increased, making it difficult to see in front of us. Cassie stepped out of the shelter.

'I think so.' Behind us, police sirens screamed through the night. 'Come on, Alice.'

She moved towards the woman and I followed. As we got closer, I saw she was dressed all in grey. It looked like she wore a silk dress and, as she came towards us, the rain stopped dancing in my ears as I heard that grey dress rustle like thunder in my head.

As the police cars roared closer to the river, the woman removed the veil she wore. Cassie and I froze together: the woman in grey had no face.

Before I could move, her hand was on mine and everything went black.

I DON'T KNOW how long the darkness lasted, but when my vision returned, my head had a herd of elephants dancing inside it. Incense filled the room, and it smelt of spices.

'Are you okay, Alice?'

Cassie sat opposite me, arms placed on her legs and unmoving. It took me a second to realise I was in a similar position. When I tried to move, nothing did.

'I'm stuck like this, Cassie. What about you?'

'I'm the same. It's like being back in the hospital room when Lucy forced me against the wall and I couldn't move.'

Lucy. Had she captured us again? Were all our efforts in Limbo for nothing?

I could move my head a little to see where we were, surrounded by walls of books.

'Maybe this is Hell's library.'

'Oh, it's nothing that exotic, girls.' A woman entered the room, her face obscured by blazing red hair, which tumbled over her shoulders. She lifted a delicate hand and swept it away, revealing piercing green eyes and saccharine sweet lips. 'Though I do have quite a lot of books which would make a fallen angel creak at the knees.'

'Who are you?' Cassie said.

The woman narrowed her eyes. 'I'm not who you were expecting at the river?'

Cassie ground her teeth so hard, it was like thunder in my ears.

'Let us go, or I'll skin you alive.'

As she laughed, the woman's red hair glistened like fireflies in the dark.

'Now, is that any way to thank the person who saved you from the coppers?'

'What do you want?' I said. 'Why are we constrained like this?'

'First things first, girls.' She pulled up a chair between us. 'My name is Hannah Pots, and you two are the Arcane sisters. Which is Alice, and who is Cassie?'

'I'm Alice. How do you know about us?'

'Well, Alice,' she removed a cigarette from her pocket and lit it, 'you two have become quite well known in the last few days.' She held a phone up so I could see it. 'Not only are the police looking for you, but most of the supernatural world is now aware of your existence.' She grinned at me as she flicked through the screen. 'There are so many marvels in modern times, but some things never change.' She pointed the phone at me. 'Have you seen how many women and girls are attacked online? Anonymous trolls accusing others of terrible untrue things, concocting lies and deceit which ruin lives.' She put the phone down and sucked on the cigarette. 'How little the world has changed since I was a girl.'

'You're not that woman from the river.'

Hannah nodded. 'That's correct, Alice. I used the Quayside Silky to bring you here. I hope she didn't frighten you too much?'

'The Quayside Silky?' I said.

Our captor let out a long line of smoke. 'Yes, Martha Wilson. Called the Quayside Silky by Newcastle residents because of the sound of her silk clothing rustling as she haunts the riverside. She normally only appears to men, but once I knew you two were arriving, I sent her out to wait for you.'

'How did you know where we'd be?' Cassie said.

Hannah smiled at my sister. Then she waved a hand in front of her head as cigarette smoke surrounded her. Her face had changed into a much younger woman, seemingly in her teens, with long blonde hair and blue eyes.

Cassie gulped. 'Claire?'

The woman with the new face nodded. 'Claire to you, many other names and faces to others across the country.'

'But... but,' Cassie struggled to speak, 'I've known you for three years.'

'And what a great time we've had, Cassie. I especially liked our nights out in Newcastle getting drunk and scaring the boys away.' She looked wistfully at me. 'It's a shame we won't get to do that again.'

Cassie was lost for words, so I spoke for her. 'Why have you been deceiving my sister for all this time?'

She waved a hand in front of her face again, and she changed back into Hannah from Claire.

'Ah, yes, sister. Cassie thought she was an only child when we first met, so I assume it must have brought her great happiness to be reunited with you, Alice.' She finished her cigarette. 'Losing a sister is the worst thing that can happen to you, so finding one must be the best feeling in the world.'

'Are you going to answer my question?'

She grinned at me. 'Do you want the short or long answer?'

'Will you let us go afterwards?'

'That all depends on if you can help me or not.'

A faint ache ran through my arms. 'Help you with what?'

Hannah reached down and removed a box from under her chair. She placed it on her knees and took off the lid.

'You have your sister, Alice, and here is mine.'

She held out the box so we could see the bones inside it.

Then that ache spread through the rest of me. 'What happened, Hannah?'

Lights flickered in the room, and I could have sworn some of the books groaned as she spoke.

'How well do you girls know your English history, particularly of this area?'

'I couldn't be bothered at school. So unless it's about methods of killing monsters, I can't help you,' Cassie said.

I glanced at my sister, knowing she was hiding her light under a bushel. I had no such qualms.

'I loved my history classes, but there is only so much you can learn.'

'Do you know of the Newcastle witch trials?'

'No,' I said as Cassie shook her head.

Hannah sighed. 'That's hardly surprising. The infamous cases at Berwick and Pendle are well known, but what happened in this city has been lost in time to many.' She placed the lid back on the box. 'But not to me. Never to me.' She looked at me. 'You know of the English Civil Wars?'

I nodded. 'Yes. Cavaliers, Roundheads, Charles I, Oliver Cromwell, and thousands of dead people.'

She put the box back under the chair. 'Indeed. The

seventeenth century was a time of turmoil, civil war, regicide and religious upheaval. It was also an age of superstition, disease and pestilence. All of these factors created a perfect recipe for social and economic uncertainty across England.

'Plague, war, and occupation by a foreign army had all visited Newcastle between 1636 and 1644. By the end of the 1640s, it was in the grip of the Puritans. The new Puritan Corporation bled the town dry through taxation, while the Puritan Regime imposed religious orthodoxy on its citizens.

'Fear of witchcraft was rife in Newcastle, and the Puritan Council sent for the one man they believed could save the town.'

I took a deep breath. 'The Witch-finder.'

Hannah got another cigarette, but didn't light it. 'The Bible states thou shalt not suffer a witch to live, but it was more a lucrative endeavour for the Witch-finder, or Witch-pricker as they were called.'

'They got paid to kill people?' Cassie said.

'They received twenty shillings a head,' Hannah said. 'Which was a considerable sum then. So a Witch-finder was summoned to travel from Scotland to Newcastle in December 1649. When he arrived, the magistrate's bellman went about the town announcing anyone with a complaint against a witch should denounce them. Then the accused would be brought to the town hall and tried. And thirty of them were.'

'So people made spurious claims without any evidence, and people were tried on that?' Cassie spat the words out.

'Yes,' Hannah said. 'And many saw this as a perfect opportunity to settle old scores or hurt those they didn't like.'

I shook my head. 'I guess some things never change.'

'The court of public opinion can sometimes lead to death, Alice, and it did then for fifteen innocent people: fourteen women accused of witchcraft and one man thought to be a wizard.'

'There were trials?' Cassie said.

A sad smile crawled across Hannah's lips. 'Perhaps some would describe them as that. The methods used were often brutal. Torture was illegal in England, but the accused would be deprived of sleep or walked for hours until they confessed. They were also subject to public humiliation, being stripped and searched for witch marks which were then "pricked" by the Witch-finder. If no blood flowed, they were guilty of witchcraft. It was not unusual for Witch-finders to employ retractable bodkins to prick their victims, thereby ensuring a guilty verdict and their fee.

'Of the thirty unfortunates accused at Newcastle, four-teen women and one man were hanged on the Town Moor in August 1650, with their remains left in unmarked graves in St Andrew's Church.'

She glanced to the floor and I understood what part she'd played in this event.

'One of your ancestors was one of those killed?'

Hannah stared at me. 'Not an ancestor, Alice, but my sister, Mary Pots.'

Cassie gasped as my heart thumped against my ribs. 'You're nearly four hundred years old?'

She held up her hands. 'Guilty as charged. There was a witch in Newcastle then, but someone who did their best for the people of that town, who used their magic to keep the crops growing and the livestock plenty and healthy. And look at how she was repaid.'

Anger seeped out of her and the air bristled with electricity. I fought against the change in the atmosphere to stay calm.

'I'm sorry for what happened to you, your sister and all the others, Hannah, but I don't see how we can help you now.'

Hannah stood and lifted her hands. As Cassie and I rose from the floor, I noticed the sparkling bracelets on our captor's wrists.

'Even with my magic, I can't resurrect the dead. For four hundred years, I've tried, have travelled across the globe, conferred with other mages, but there was never anything capable of bringing my sister back.' She glanced at Cassie, and then me. 'Until I learnt of the Arcane sisters and what is in their blood.'

Cassie glared at her. 'You've known what I am since we met; since you deceived me?'

'No, Cassie, I wasn't aware of how special you were then. I spend a lot of time with abandoned children, especially girls, to see if I can help them, and when I met you, I realised you were different from the others. But I didn't know how different until now.'

'You used her,' I said. 'You're no different to any other manipulator.'

'I can understand your anger, Alice, but you must recognise I'd do anything for my sister. I'm sure you would for yours.'

I struggled to move as we floated five feet off the ground, but it was no use.

'Why do you think we can help you? We're not witches.'

She beamed at me. 'You're much better than that, Alice. Witches have to use objects to create their magic, but your power is inside you. It's natural, passed down directly from the Creator. That is what will bring my Mary back to me.'

'Okay, okay.' I watched the sparkle of her bracelets increase, until they were like tiny disco lights on her wrists. 'I'm sure Cassie and I can spare a few drops each. We'll give you that, and then you can let us go.'

Hannah bent her fingers into a fist and an invisible pressure squeezed against my chest.

'I'm sorry, Alice, but it won't work like that. My sister has been nothing but bones for four centuries, and it will take all of your and Cassie's blood to return her to life.'

'You're mad,' Cassie said.

'Possibly,' the witch said. 'But my love is greater than any madness that might possess me.'

I reached deep inside me, searching for the strength I'd had in Limbo, sensing something hiding within me.

'You haven't thought this through, Hannah. If those bones are all you have left of Mary, then our blood could destroy them forever.'

She peered at me. 'What do you mean, child?'

'Cassie and I visited a demon and angel in Hollywood. Do you know about that?'

Fear crept across her face for the first time. 'The actors? It was you who killed them?'

'It wasn't intentional. But they tried to drink from our bodies, and it was that which poisoned them. And if it did that to an angel and demon, what will our blood do to four-hundred-year-old bones?'

The fear didn't leave her as she raised one hand to her face. The bracelet had stopped shimmering and was now only a dull echo. The strain around my body had lessened and I'd dropped closer to the carpet.

'Without her bones, there will be no way to resurrect my sister.'

I was that low, I could touch the floor with my toes. 'It's not worth the risk, Hannah. Let us go, and I promise that Cassie and I will help you find a way to bring back Mary.'

She snapped her head to me and glared. 'No. You have the blood of the divine in you, direct descendants of the Creator. Life will come from you and return my sister to me.'

Her confidence had returned with her anger, but it was too late. That slight hesitation had freed me and my feet were on the ground again. So I stepped forward and punched her hard in the gut.

Hannah crumpled to the carpet, the light around her wrists gone now. I looked at Cassie and smiled. But we didn't have any time to congratulate ourselves.

A giant fist hit the side of my head, and the last thing I saw was Hannah lying next to me before I blacked out.

I must have fallen through time. My hands were younger, smaller, digging into the dirt and grass around me; the air stank of chemicals and fresh blood. An electricity generator hummed nearby. The glass sticking out of my knee vibrated in sequence with the generator, shivers of pain speeding through my body. I was six years old again, and I knew what would happen next.

'Get up, girl.'

Fingers as thick as jumbo sausages grabbed the nape of my neck and dragged me across the grass. This is my first memory, the one which never leaves or fades. My shoes dug into the ground, thin legs straining against empty air. It would be a failed attempt to stop this woman from taking me back to the care home she ran with her fundamentalist husband. This was the first time I'd run away, but it wouldn't be the last.

'You're hurting me.' I didn't scream or shout, ignoring the pain to stare at her tortured face. Her eyes were like large cracked eggs, all runny and a reminder of something which once lived. Bitterness burned inside her scowl.

'This is your own fault, child.' She threw me to the side, up against the wall around the house. Its brutal and blank surface stared at me. I hadn't got far from the place when I'd tripped and landed on the broken bottle. 'This is God's punishment.' She was about to start her sermon. Blood trickled down my leg as I stuck my fingers in my ears. I shut her and the rest of the world out. It was a practice I got used to as I grew older and wiser. She towered over me, rage bursting from her in great lumps and jagged lines, which made her look much older than she was. I couldn't hear what she said.

But then I could.

'Are you listening, Ms Valentine?'

My eyes flickered open and I tried to adjust to the harsh artificial light. 'What?'

My past disappeared, replaced by an uncomfortable present. The woman sitting opposite was smartly dressed and a perfect example of tranquillity: she was a world away from that first memory, but I recognised something behind this woman's eyes similar to that fundamentalism. She pushed a photograph across the table.

'Do you recognise this boy?'

I stared down at the image as a movement caught my eye. There was someone else there, but I concentrated on the photo. It was dark and a little blurry, but I recognised it instantly: a body floating in the lake. It seemed like a lifetime away. I lifted my head, staring past her and at the heavyset man in the corner.

'I don't know who that it is.' It was the truth.

The woman retrieved the image. 'Are you sure? Because we have a witness who places you at the scene of this murder.'

My heart leapt. 'A witness?' That meant Akemi was

okay. I leant into the chair and relaxed a little, breathing slowly. There was a low ache at the back of my neck, and my knee throbbed.

'Do you want to tell us what happened?' She framed it as a question, but it sounded more like a demand. There was no point denying I was there.

'He attacked us and dragged me into the lake. His hands were around my throat, drowning me when something stopped him. When I climbed out of the water, he was dead, and I was on my own. I left and went home.'

'Our witness confirms your story of self-defence, but why didn't you report it to the police?'

I scoured my mind for an adequate response. I grabbed the glass of water in front of me and drank half of it.

'I was scared, wasn't thinking straight. I needed to go to my flat, get out my wet clothes. Before I knew it, I was asleep. And then...'

What could I say about a zombie attack?

She pushed another photo my way.

'Do you recognise this?'

It was hard not to. 'That's my flat.'

'Do you know what the stain on the floor is?'

I picked up the picture, a sudden sensation of lethargy creeping through my fingers. Sweat dripped from my head and into my eyes. The heat had arrived from nowhere. She was dressed in a suit and shirt and was as cold as ice. The man in the corner, his face hidden by the shadows, mumbled to himself. I wiped the damp from my eyes and gazed into the image of my previous life.

'I spilt some beer there a few days ago.'

Her expression cracked a little with the first sign of emotion.

'That seems strange considering a DNA test of the

liquid came back as the remains of your neighbours, Bob Jones and Terry Marr.' I placed my hand on the table, unable to move it any further. 'There are twelve flats in that block. Including you, thirty-three people lived there.'

'Lived?' My heart sank. I'd hoped the zombie thing had only affected a few people.

'You're the only survivor. Don't you find that strange, Ms Valentine?'

'I don't know what happened there. I was lucky to escape with my life.'

'And how did you do that?' Her gaze cut right through me.

I tried to move my hands, but it was as if they were glued to the table, and my legs appeared to contain liquid cement.

'What happened to the women I was with?' I didn't care about the witch, but where was Cassie?

'What happened at your flat in Middlesbrough, Ms Valentine? Why did you say you were lucky to escape with your life?'

'There was an attack on the building. I heard my neighbours screaming and ran out as fast as I could.' The image of Bob and Terry, of their faces collapsing into melting flesh, continued to lurk at the back of my head.

She stared at me and I couldn't tell if she believed me or not.

'How did you get from there to Newcastle?'

That was a good question, but I could hardly tell her my lookalike sister used a magical knife to cut through space and bring us here. Here? Were we still in Newcastle? Were these people really the police?

I tried to shrug my shoulders, but they wouldn't move.

Perhaps it was an after effect of what Hannah had done to me.

'It was all a blur. I staggered to the station and got the first train here.'

'That was two days ago. Where have you been since then?'

'I was staying with friends. What's happened to them?'

She didn't answer, got up and nodded to the faceless man in the corner. Then she exited the room and left me alone with him. He lit a cigarette and took the seat she'd vacated.

He was built like a bodybuilder, physique bursting against the pin-striped suit he wore. He blew smoke into the air where it circled, ready to strike. He was as bald as an egg, with small brown eyes hidden inside dark skin. But I saw another colour hiding behind them and had a sudden realisation this was no ordinary police station.

'My name is Captain Aziz, and this is my investigation.'

The only part of me capable of moving was my mouth. 'You're a demon.'

The purple replaced the brown in his eyes and glistened.

'I am the Lord of this territory.'

I glanced at the empty glass. 'The water was drugged?'

He took another drag on the cigarette. 'It was something to keep you pliable while I decide what to do with you and your sister.'

'Where is she?' I tried to muster some anger, but it was impossible, fatigue consuming my muscle and bone.

'She's being interviewed like you are. The more you cooperate, the easier it will be for both of you.'

'How did you know where we'd be?'

He tapped his nose. 'Our informants are everywhere. It's one of the many benefits to working for the police.'

'What happened to Hannah?' Anger tried to push its way up from my gut, but all I got was an irritating rumble.

'The witch is not your concern.' His smile looked wrong, as if the muscles in his face were fighting against moving anywhere but down.

'Was it you who issued the contract on us?' If I kept him talking, the drug might wear off sooner rather than later.

He finished the cigarette and dropped it into the glass I'd been foolish enough to drink from.

'No. Some locals were unhappy with your sister's activities, so they wanted her caught, and then they discovered there are two of you. That meant a double reward for some of them. Greed isn't only a human weakness.'

'How did they know where I lived?'

'You had werewolf blood on you, and that is easy to track, but your exploits in the café scared a few of them, so they instructed a mage to infect your building.' He shook his head and anger rippled through his flesh. 'The magic they used was too strong; the infected were supposed to contain you, but we ended up with that.' He slammed his hand on to the photo of my flat. 'And I've had to deal with the fallout ever since, not helped by the two of you disappearing from the face of the planet. But now you're here, under my control.'

I didn't care about his veiled threats. 'Do you know how we get into Hell?'

His laugh was full-throttled and hearty, like someone at the front of a comedy show who'd heard the greatest joke ever written.

'And why would you want to go there?'

I strained at invisible chains, but my body wouldn't budge. I went for bravado.

'We are the Children of the Nephilim and we will rescue our mother from your Queen.'

He scratched his head and peered at me in surprise.

'The Nephilim died thousands of years ago, so whoever said that lied to you. And I follow no rule but my own.'

'Doesn't Lucy rule over Hell and its demons while Michael leads the angels and looks after Heaven when God is on holiday?'

Aziz stood, peering into the mirror behind me. The chair was stuck to my body. He strode around me - sturdy, muscular legs, but with a light touch - until he stopped and put his hands on my shoulders. He leant down to whisper into my ear. He smelt of Armani perfume for men.

'God is a fiction created to scare children and the witless.' His fingers pressed into my flesh and my body throbbed. 'I and many like me have no interest in the squabbles of archangels, but my life here is too good to have it interrupted by their interminable conflicts.'

My body ached from the pressure he put on me.

'Michael wants to wipe out humanity and use my sister and me to do it.'

I didn't know why I blurted out the words, but I did. Maybe it was to throw him off balance. He spun me around in the chair and frowned at me, his eyes full of purple. Heat blazed from them.

'How would the two of you be capable of that?'

Confusion rippled through his face, that and a tinge of fear.

'I told you: we're the Children of the Nephilim. Apparently, that's a big deal.'

The Demon Lord Aziz gazed into me, and what I saw behind his shimmering purple didn't look too happy.

'Even if they existed, the Children of the Nephilim are nothing special, only the offspring of angels and humans. Some want your sister dead because of what she's done.' He glared at me. 'And now both of you are a hindrance to keeping the likes of me hidden from the human world. Only your disappearance will return things to normal. I'm sorry.'

'I don't believe you're sorry at all, Aziz. I think you and your demon thugs enjoy hurting people like me.' I glanced around the room. 'And I guess you enjoy your position of power here in the police, and my sister and I are a threat to that.'

He snorted laughter at me. 'Yes, child, two teenage girls worry me greatly.'

'Your boss, Lucy, told me that Cassie and I have the potential to rival God. So maybe that's what you're scared of, and this little charade is just to ease your masculine sensibilities.'

He ran his fingers across my skin, touching my lips and pressing into my gums.

'Well, child, if that's the case, weapons of mass destruction should be dismantled before they blow up.' He used his hand to force my mouth open as wide as possible. Agony shot through my jaw, spiralling over my teeth like someone hammering on to piano keys. He bent down and peered into my throat. 'So, you're saying there's no soul down there. That's a shame.' He let go and my jaw snapped shut. The drug numbed part of my pain, but not all of it, my face feeling as if lead weights lived there.

'How does this body wearing thing work for demons and angels?' My tongue was the only bit I could move, brushing it over my gums and the inside of my mouth.

There was a faint taste of blood. I strained against my fingers and toes with no success.

'Do you think this information will help you when you get to Hell?' He sat opposite me again, his hand drumming on the table.

'Knowledge is power.' If he was considering me reaching Hell, then he might let us go.

His grin consumed all of his head. 'We crawl up inside you and devour your soul at our leisure from your insides. It is most pleasant, but not for the human host. Their death can take years, their minds imprisoned behind a demon wall, watching and suffering as we inhabit their flesh suits.' He licked his lips as he spoke. 'Would you like me to show you?'

I pushed and pulled at the front of my mind, heat searing the sides of my skull. My head twitched, and so did my arms. I leant towards him as confusion gripped his eyes.

'I think you should, Aziz, because the last thing which tried to eat my soul collapsed to the floor in what looked like excruciating agony.' My feet scraped against the ground and the chair legs screeched as they moved.

Aziz pulled back from the table, hands high in front of him in a defensive posture. Silence cut the air, only shattered by the entrance of the plainclothes policewoman from before. She handed him a mobile phone.

'You need to see the news; we've got bigger problems than two waifs.'

My fingers were becoming looser, but I didn't move them, reluctant to let my captors see how free I was. Aziz stared at the screen with wide eyes.

'Did your favourite contestant get kicked off X *Factor*?' I flexed my legs and considered if I could take them both together. He turned the phone towards me.

'Do you know anything about this?'

I peered at the device, a multitude of websites dominated by the same word.

War!

'What does this mean?' My bones tingled.

Aziz changed the display to a single image of a ship flying the US flag. It looked like an aircraft carrier.

'Have you been hiding under a rock for the last twenty-four hours? Taiwan has come to a standstill after a barrage of cyberattacks cut its access to water and power. US satellites have also been affected. The Chinese navy is blockading the island, during which they sunk an American navy ship with all lives on board lost.'

I stared at the headlines again and thought of Akemi. 'And now the American's have declared war?' All my problems seemed so far away.

'It didn't take them long. And our government, with our special relationship, are supporting them. The missiles could fly before we leave this room.'

All my strength leaked out of me. 'Why would I have anything to do with this?' Was it all a trick?

'You claim to be the Children of the Nephilim, and it is said the Children of the Nephilim will bring about the end of everything. This is one way of doing it.'

I let the pain wash over me. 'Why don't you and your friends get under the skin of these people and stop this madness?'

His shoulders slumped into the chair, the width of them making the plastic squeak.

'I wish it was that simple. Every major government in the world performs daily tests on those in charge to catch out monsters in human flesh suits.'

'They can do that?' It took a second for the new information to sink in, my lips trembling at the sides.

'A minority of humans have known about us for centuries, and some of your leaders know how to seek us out when we hide inside fleshy forms. That is why the likes of me hang around in people like this.' He ran his fingers across his chin. 'It makes for an easier life.'

I'd fixed my eyes on him so much, I didn't see the woman moving behind me. As I flexed my hands and legs, ready to move, she stuck something sharp into my neck. A cold liquid swam deep into my veins, sinking through skin and sinew, depositing stupor into every part of my body. I flopped into the back of the chair.

'Shall we call a meeting of the Council about this?' Her voice trembled through the new fog invading my brain.

'It's too late for us to do anything about it now; all we can do is look after ourselves.' He walked towards me, lifting my jaw and peering into my eyes. 'These girls came here seeking an entrance into Hell. I think it's time we sent them there the traditional way. Dispose of them by any method you see fit, but make sure there are no bodies to find.'

He stroked my cheek and my flesh struggled against the drug, freezing me into the chair. He turned and left the room.

'I will enjoy this,' she said before punching me in the nose.

I fell to the floor, my limbs numb to the pain as I hit the ground.

7 TOILER ON THE SEA

I was head first in filth, a nose full of mud and mouth gobbing out grass. Spitting rain fell from above. The movement had returned to my body, if only fleetingly. My hands were in damp earth when I pushed myself up, face staring into the night sky. A flock of seagulls hovered above my aching limbs, chattering away as if mocking me. To my right stood one bird, dancing in the dirt. It was a peculiar sight to observe until I realised it was pulling a worm from the soil. It flew off with the invertebrate between its claws as I tried to contain the throbbing in my skull.

'Can you move?' Cassie's voice shook me back into the moment. She was a few feet away, also lying on the ground, her arms stuck to her side.

I lifted my torso, the only part of me able to move, my legs and arms frozen.

'A little. Are you okay?'

'Apart from being pissed off, I'll live.' Blazing anger illuminated her eyes. 'Where are we?'

The sea was in front of me, salty air drifting over from

the horizon, hovering above the dark blue water. It was diffi-cult to shift my shoulder, but I did, twisting my head to the side and peering at the gravestones and the ruins rising behind me.

'Are we in Whitby?' Did we somehow transport ourselves there without realising it?

'You're a long way from there, girls.'

The smartly dressed policewoman strode forward, flanked by half a dozen others, all of whom carried swords at their sides. The woman was applying bright yellow gloss to her lips.

I lifted my fingers to my neck, examining the fresh bruise there.

'You drugged me and brought us here; why?'

'Lord Aziz and I have our doubts about your claims to be the Children of the Nephilim, but there is something different about you which we need to contain.'

'It's a strange place for murder.'

'You won't die, girls; not yet, anyway. Your destination is there.' She pointed towards the sea. I strained my eyes, settling on the hole in the earth I'd missed before.

'You dug one grave for two?' Cassie lifted, resting her knees in the dirt.

'It's best to have you both in the same place, and this is close enough to the consecrated ground to keep the rest of us safe from whatever you are.'

I moved my gaze from the grave and returned it to the graveyard and the ruins beyond it.

'Are we still in Newcastle?'

'Not quite. This is Tynemouth Priory, about seventy miles along the coast from Whitby.'

As I focused on her, hands grabbed my shoulders and

dragged me across the ground, my frozen limbs slipping through mud and rain. Two more thugs did the same to Cassie. I didn't shout or struggle, my mind working overtime trying to construct a way out of our mess.

They threw us on to the verge of what would soon be our family grave. As I raised my head from the grass, a pair of tiny lights like the smallest eyes in existence stared at me from the edge of the cliff-top. I blinked twice, my jaw-dropping to see a gnome peering back at me. Then it ran away before anyone else noticed it.

'When I get out of this, you'll be the first person I find and kill.' Cassie hurled the words at the woman as the police officer placed her foot on my sister's chest. Her reply to the threat was to kick Cassie into the hole.

'You'll die in there, or the both of you will talk to the worms for a long time.' Her foot was on my stomach.

'If she doesn't do it, I will.' I could move my hands and my feet, but it was too late as she kicked me into the grave. I landed with a thump on top of Cassie, my face pushed up to hers. We struggled against each other, our breathing coming in rapid bursts. Dirt fell on to my back as laughter came from above.

Cassie spat grass from her lips. 'So, what do we do now?' She appeared far more relaxed than I was. More clumps of mud rained down on us.

'Can you move properly?'

I only had one idea in mind. Cassie pressed her hands into my hips and moved her legs from side to side.

'I think so, but it's a ten-foot hole they've dropped us into. If we try to climb out of it, they'll swot us back with those swords they have.'

'You'll be able to scramble out unobstructed once you

throw me from here.' I smiled a little as confusion spread across her face.

'And how will I do that, dear Sister?' The dirt continued to cover me. We were running out of time.

'Remember when we fought the harpies in Limbo, how strong you felt? We need to find that strength again, so you'll push while I spring up at the same moment. I know where they are at the edge. I'll take them out as I reach the top and keep them occupied while you get out of this pit.'

She shook her head. 'And where do we get that strength from, Alice? My body is still riddled with whatever that witch did to us, as well as the drugs the demons shot us full of.' It was the first time I'd seen her despondent.

I reached across and took her hand. 'Think back to us in Limbo and those harpies, how we felt when they attacked, and how we reacted. We're still the same two people. Whatever was in us then is in us now. No witchcraft or pharmaceuticals can take away our heritage.' I gripped her fingers. 'We're not doing this for us, Cassie; we're doing it to rescue our mother.'

She grinned and nodded. Cassie twisted underneath me, her arms and legs flexing against mine.

'On three,' she said.

We stretched and spoke together. 'One, two, three.'

I flung my body up as she shoved with all her might. I was like a balloon when the air is suddenly released from it and it shoots up into the sky, my torso twisting as I reached the edge. There were two of them shovelling. I caught one across the face with my arm, the other with my outstretched foot into their neck.

My feet hit the ground. Rolling to the side, I sprung up in one go. Between me and the cemetery were the other four and the woman, all of their astonished eyes staring at me. Before they could move or do anything, there was the sound of crushed bones behind me.

'That was a great plan, Alice.'

Cassie was with me, a bloodied spade in her hand. Next to her were the headless corpses of the two who'd tried to bury us.

The policewoman watched as the others drew their swords.

I pulled dirt from my mouth. 'Is this a medieval battle re-enactment?'

Confidence surged through me. Moonlight bounced off the sea and shot over our heads, landing on their blades; a golden haze shimmered around them. We were without our knives, but I didn't care about being outnumbered and outgunned.

I turned to Cassie.

'Let's use the Blade of Reality.' I wasn't sure if I meant to escape or for destruction. She pursed her lips in a grimace.

'I lost it at the station. The police attacked me at the same time they grabbed you. It must have fallen from my pocket during the fight because it wasn't there when we ran.'

The golden glow around the swords grew brighter.

'And you're only telling me this now?'

'We've been quite busy since then. Or knocked out.'

'Kai won't be happy with that.' I wasn't happy with it. And then things got worse.

The golden shimmer transformed into full-blown flames. So now we had burning swords to deal with.

'A fiery death will be much worse than being buried alive, girls, believe me.' The only thing brighter than those blazing blades was the policewoman's grin.

'Take this.' Cassie handed me the bloodied spade, and then picked up the other one from the ground.

I grabbed it from her. 'Second-hand shovels against flaming swords; what's to worry about?'

I gripped the handle and waited for our opponents to make the first move. The flock of seagulls had scarpered away as soon as the fire spread through the metal. We stared at our abductors with the sound of the flames in the air.

The woman stood between her thugs and I wondered if they were waiting for her to give them a signal. Then, they spun the swords in an arc by their sides as if recreating a synchronised movement. It was impressive and distracting. As I flexed my leg muscles, the four ran at us together, two towards me, while the others sprinted for Cassie. I waited for the adrenaline to come, for that same energy that had infected me when fighting the harpies.

But nothing happened.

Two arcs of flaming metal descended for my head, my reflexes as slow as they'd ever been. Sparks flew at me, the air burning with smoke, my throat as dry as the desert.

Cassie pushed me to the side, both of us stumbling from the attack.

'Wake up, Alice!' she screamed at me. We ran from the priory, heading towards the drop to the sea, dashing for a good thirty seconds. Death at our backs and death ahead; there was no choice but to fight.

At least our flight had separated the group. They couldn't have trained to work as a unit, our speed having split them up. There were two in front, with the others struggling to catch up. Perhaps those swords were heavier than they looked.

Cassie and I stopped to face the two closest to us. We lifted the shovels in unison, raising them to block the burning orange metal as it headed for our faces. Wood met fire, scattering splinters and flames together into the darkness. I stepped back, pulled the spade down and jabbed into my attacker's gut before he could move. Then I rammed it into the other guy as he readied to chop at Cassie's head. We fled as they recovered and their colleagues joined them.

'We're running into a dead end, Alice.'

Cassie's voice was high, breath bursting from her lungs. Someone had plugged a thousand-watt generator into my heart. We were maybe fifty yards ahead of our pursuers.

'Then we must make a stand here.'

My feet froze on the edge of the cliff, my head twisting to glance at the surf below. My ears picked out the sounds of the sea somewhere in the dark, waves booming against rocks. How far was it? Was it a drop that would kill?

My head swivelled back as the heat seared towards me. I parried the hot metal with the cold steel of my shovel, pulling it away to prevent the other sword from crashing into my skull. I was too late, the fire brushing my fingers, the flames cutting into my palm as I lifted my hand. I fell and rolled to the edge. An inferno burnt through my smoking skin as I beat out the flames in the grass.

The demon loomed above me, ready to bring down the sword again one final time.

Cassie screamed, her arm aflame as she swung her spade into the neck of the thug standing over me. Decapitation was instantaneous, his head flying from the shoulders into the depths of the sea. The three remaining demons inched back from us. Cassie continued to burn, her face contorted in agony. She pulled me up with her free hand. My weapon was splintered and useless. The heat coming off her was uncomfortable, even for me.

'Kill them now.' The woman glared as she commanded

her servants to murder. And then I saw the fire at her neck, flames which must have jumped from Cassie's arm and on to her. She grimaced as she used her hand to quash the burning at her throat.

I only had one good hand, and half of Cassie was on fire. There was no way we could defend ourselves against them. I'd been wrong about our potential, had assumed what we'd felt in Limbo would come back, but it hadn't. There was only one choice left for us.

'We have to jump into the sea, Cassie.'

She peered at me through the smoke. 'I can't swim, Alice.'

From somewhere, a laugh escaped me.

'Don't worry. The fall will probably kill you.'

As we laughed together, the demons charged at us with their flaming weapons in front of them. I turned from them, held on to Cassie, and we leapt into the dark.

It seemed an age as we fell into the abyss.

Gravity pulled my fingers from Cassie's as we hit an inky brick wall of liquid concrete. The sea sucked me down into its cold embrace, water flooding my eyes and mouth, my hands clutching at my throat as my lungs struggled to work. Ghostly limbs dragged at me as I sank further and further. There was nothing to see in the darkness, no sign of the sister I'd only recently discovered.

They say your life flashes before you when you're on the verge of death, but all I got was the last few days starting with my walk through that park: the werewolf boy face down in the water; meeting my identical twin sister; the wolf pack in the café; my neighbours transforming into liquid zombies; a road trip to Lindisfarne and a cult collecting supernatural creatures; Kai and the Impossible Palace; the mermaids of Staithes; chatting with Dracula;

befriending Medusa; inadvertently poisoning the angel and demon couple of Hollywood; travelling through time; seeing my mother; and being attacked by two archangels; learning I'm a Child of the Nephilim; a visit to Limbo; being snatched by a witch, and then abducted by a Demon Lord. And all of this while the world appeared to be hovering on the brink of war.

And that made me think of Akemi again. If I'd stayed with her inside the university bar, would any of this have happened? Was she really on Teesside working secretly for the Taiwanese nuclear programme? Would that be any stranger than everything I'd seen since she ran away from me in the park?

Was everything that had happened my fault?

Perhaps it would be easier to sink into the watery void.

A hand flashed into mine, flesh linking into the recent scar on my palm. Then I was moving up towards the light, a bright dot floating beyond the horizon. I gasped for air as my head burst through the water and stared at the moon smiling at me. My saviour held me in her arms and had stopped burning.

'Stay awake, Alice.' She must have shouted at me, the way her eyes bulged and mouth gaped, but it appeared like a whisper in my ears. 'I've got you, but I need you to keep us afloat.'

I went to say something, but we both sank below the sea again, with the water invading my mouth. I tried to stay with her, but the waves were too strong and they pulled us apart.

Cassie's mouth was open, her eyes wide as the current took her from me.

It would have been so easy just to let go and follow her down.

So I did. But only to grab her hand and haul her up with me above the water.

We burst forth and took great gulps of air. My hands were around Cassie's waist as I manoeuvred on to my back to keep us afloat. And then I heard the sound of the blaring horn.

'There's a siren in the ocean.'

Saltwater sputtered from my lips. I gazed at the moon and the stars with my arms around Cassie's. A large shadow blocked out the sky and loomed over us. What new demon horror did we have to deal with now?

Mist drifted across me, obscuring my view, before departing as quickly as it had arrived. The water chilled my bones, and the air sliced at my face. A strange red light glowed in front of us, leading the way for the titanic mast pointing through the last of the sea fret. It was a ship, but not one the likes of which I'd ever seen, apart from in history books and adventure tales of pirates. It was huge, dwarfing the horizon, wavering in the moonlight and glowing.

As it approached, I made out the sails flapping against the flaky wooden masts, and the menacing shadows standing at the sides. Waves crashed around the vessel but, impossibly, avoided us as we floated transfixed in the sea. If this was our doom, there was no escaping it.

Cassie pushed her wet face into mine. 'Are you seeing this?'

I kissed her lightly on the chin, a damp expression of family love I never thought I'd experience.

'Well, we need a lift.'

The ship was close enough for us to realise those looming shadows were flickering apparitions of ghastly humans. Their ghostly faces screamed terror and horror in equal measure. Standing in the middle of them must have been their captain, a nightmarish vision with a face made from wrinkled parchment and eyes burning yellow and red. A blue cape flowed behind him high into the winds, the colour matching his trousers and contrasting with the vivid scarlet of a sizeable crimson scarf tied around his waist, which blew from his side like vampirish nails stretching out for death. He stepped from view, and someone threw a makeshift ladder over the edge.

My body shivered in the water. My hair splattered against my forehead, my eyes fixed on Cassie.

'We either stay here and freeze or climb up there and see what awaits us.'

We crawled to the ship, arms pushing hard against the sea, fighting the urge to turn away and swim into nothingness. I got my hand on the rope first, dragging my aching bones up the ladder one rung at a time. Cassie followed. We had no weapons and no energy beyond the minimum to get on board the vessel.

It was only as we reached the top and I glanced back that I saw Cassie had lost her jacket, which had burnt against her flesh. The sleeve of her shirt appeared stuck to her arm. The scar on my wrist throbbed as I stepped on to the deck.

In my mind, we were ready for anything, even though my body was screaming for sleep. The captain stood in the middle of the ship, his crew on either side of him. Ancient enmity seeped from them like cheap cologne dripping off nightclub bouncers.

'What do you want?'

My teeth chattered and my lips shivered as I spoke. I held on to Cassie to stop my legs from buckling under me.

The captain opened his mouth, but the voice came from behind him, a feminine lilt I recognised at once.

'I'm sorry I couldn't get here sooner, girls, but I didn't know you were in trouble until a few hours ago, and it isn't easy to book passage on a ghost ship at the last minute.'

8 CHILDREN OF THE SEA

Kai stepped from the shadows, her svelte ballerina-like figure gliding towards us. Cassie and I ran in stereo to throw our arms around the Warwitch. I let go of her once my heart stopped beating like a jackhammer. The rain had dissipated into nothing, but my hand throbbed.

'What are you doing here?'

Her smile was warm enough to light up my flesh. 'We need to get you into some dry clothes, and then I'll tell you all about it.' She turned to the captain and nodded at him; he lifted a ghostly arm and pointed to the door leading below decks. Kai grabbed our hands and dragged us there. 'I don't know what garments van der Decken has here, but they have to be better than what you're wearing.'

She pushed the door open and took us downstairs, along a narrow corridor, and into a cabin large enough to be the captain's quarters. It was spotlessly clean and appeared as if no one had lived there for a long time.

I dragged the jacket from my weary torso and tossed it on to the floor.

'What is this place?'

Kai was busy opening cupboards and throwing clothing over the sofas dotted around the room.

'This is the *Flying Dutchman* and the gentleman upstairs is Captain Hendrick van der Decken. He owes me a favour, so he'll take you wherever you want to go.'

Cassie had her back to us as she removed her shirt. I only glimpsed her fire-damaged arm, parts of her skin all shrivelled and burnt. I couldn't imagine how painful it must have been. We dressed in silence, selecting shirts, jackets and trousers which were old and warm to the touch. It didn't matter we looked like rejects from a terrible pirate show.

Cassie smoothed out the wrinkles in her top and faced Kai.

'Isn't the *Flying Dutchman* a cursed ship condemned to sail the oceans for eternity, with a ghostly crew of dead men bringing death to all who see them?'

Kai scrunched her eyes in a reflective mood. 'Yes, but that doesn't apply to friends like me. As soon as I heard you were in trouble, I summoned Captain van der Decken to Whitby, and we sped along the coast to here. The one good thing about being in charge of a ghost ship is how supernaturally quick it can travel across the water.'

I examined the surrounding trinkets, picking up an antique compass and peering at the row of skulls placed on a table at the back of the room.

'How did you know we were in trouble?'

The Warwitch plumped herself between the piles of discarded clothes on the largest sofa.

'The Gorgon messaged me, said it worried her when you never texted her from Newcastle. I wouldn't have known where you were if those idiots hadn't taken you to Tynemouth Priory. We priory guardians have a network across the country and always share unusual activity in our group. I'd told George about you two, and he informed me as soon as you arrived on the grounds. I was already aboard this ship, and Captain van der Decken got us up the coast in record time, but not quick enough to stop both of you from jumping into the ocean. Luckily, we found you before it was too late.'

My phone was drying out on the side, thankfully not lost to the sea. I grabbed it and turned to Kai.

'Is your friend George a gnome?'

She grinned at me. 'He's small, but perfectly formed. Did you see him?'

'Yes, I think so, just before those goons threw us into the grave.' I texted Medusa as I spoke.

Cassie plopped her body next to Kai. 'So, apart from you, we owe our lives to a Gorgon, a ghost, and a gnome?'

Kai clapped her hands together. 'Isn't it great? Now tell me everything that's happened since you left Whitby.'

We took it in turns to relay those events, including the loss of the Blade of Reality, which didn't go down well. All the time, I was listening to the sound of ghostly footsteps above our heads.

A thought closer to home came to me.

'Is the world at war yet?'

Kai smiled. 'It appears as if some common sense has returned to humanity. World leaders are trying to talk conciliation to the US and China, but everyone is still on tenterhooks. The press has published leaks stating that Prime Minister Howard is in constant contact with the American president, Daniel Cross, to make sure he doesn't do anything stupid.'

I searched my brain for those images of Cross I'd had during his victory speech, picturing a handsome man a lot younger than his predecessors. His inauguration was less than a year ago, and it was hard at that time, even for me, not to get caught up in the sense of positive change which spread across the US and the world. How things had changed since then; in more ways than one.

'Do you think there's a supernatural element involved in this?'

Kai scratched at her chin. 'You mean a deliberate move by a Celestial to rain nuclear fire down on the planet? I suppose it's possible, but I can't see what the point of it would be. Celestials enjoy feeding off human souls; you won't get that if most of the population is dead.'

'So, what do we do now?' Sleep, my body said to me.

'It would appear we're no further forward in finding your mother, and we don't have the Blade of Reality anymore.' Kai didn't hide the disappointment in her voice.

A surge of heat infected the cabin. I pulled at the neck of my shirt and puffed out my cheeks exaggeratedly.

'I need some fresh air.'

Cassie gave me a curious stare. 'You want to go back up top with the ghosts?'

I strode towards the door, enjoying the sensation of dry clothes brushing against my skin.

'It might clear our heads regarding what to do next.'

They followed me up the stairs, the salty sea breeze bringing a welcome chill to my bones. I was tired, but I couldn't sleep because we needed a plan of action before I could relax. The deck was empty as I stepped on to it, the *Flying Dutchman's* spirit crew having vanished into the night. The captain was there, leaning over the side with his head stuck across the edge like a pointer dog. His face was wrinkled parchment shimmering in the wind's howl, a wail which appeared to be surrounding only him. His nose twitched from side to side curiously.

I grabbed Kai's arm. 'What's he doing?'

'He's sniffing out death.'

'What?' Cassie and I said together.

Watery sadness filled Kai's eyes. 'The poor captain is possessed to seek fellow seafarers who are equally cursed.'

'You mean he sniffs out the aroma of those about to die at sea?'

Kai slipped from my grasp. 'Those about to die or who are recently perished and need transportation along the next part of their journey. It's his eternal burden.'

'Who placed this curse on him and his crew, and why?' Was that a hint of pity I detected in Cassie?

'Some say the captain offended God, and this is Divine punishment,' Kai said.

'This would be the same God who tried to kill our mother?' It was only anger in Cassie's voice now.

'The same.'

'The one who is returning to Earth to cleanse it of humanity.' The wind brushed a dark hair across her face and she left it there. 'I look forward to meeting such a being.'

Cassie appeared to be preparing herself for a fight, but I had no interest in a Divine Creator at this moment. Watching the ghostly captain sniffing out death had given me an idea.

'We need a Hellhound.'

Kai and Cassie stared at me in confusion.

'Are you after a pet, Sister?'

'To find a gateway into Hell and rescue our mother, we want something born in its fiery bowels that can track its way back.' I faced Kai. 'What do you know of Hellhounds?'

The Warwitch scratched her head and scrunched her eyes.

'Hellhounds used to guard the places of the dead before demons tamed them for their needs, using them as instruments of punishment for both the living and the deceased. They are the Bearer of Death, as dark as coal and smelling of burning brimstone. Their eyes are deep, bright, and almost glowing red. They have razor-sharp teeth, super strength and speed, and are associated with graveyards and the underworld. According to legend, seeing one leads to a person's demise. I have met only one such creature, the Cù-sìth, and it's near here.'

Her words sparked life back into my weary limbs. 'This Hellhound is in England?'

She shook her head. 'The Cù-sìth is in the Scottish Highlands.'

The ghostly captain had turned away from his search and stared at us. I ignored his gaze.

'So we can take this ship up the coast and into Scotland?'

Kai didn't look too happy at the prospect. 'We can, but we have two problems to deal with.'

I feared no potential difficulties. 'What are they?'

Kai removed her phone and handed it to me. 'This is the latest news.'

'Crap.' I peered at the screen in disbelief before handing it to Cassie. She shook her head and grimaced, scanning the story of the police searching for two sisters for the murder of the boy in the park.

'That's a terrible photo of me they got from my juvenile record. You look terrified staring into the camera, Alice.'

'It's from the ID photos Artemis took of me.' I resisted

the urge to ask Cassie about her juvenile record and addressed Kai. 'What's the other problem?'

'The Cù-sìth is a fearsome beast, possessed of shaggy dark green fur and the size of a cow, but that is nothing compared to the one who controls it.'

'And who is that?' Cassie said.

An icy gust swept across the deck and threatened to blow us away. I clung to the side of the ship as huge waves bounced against the wood below. Kai pushed damp strands of hair from her eyes as she spoke.

'Her name is Vika Vistala, and she is a Baobhan Sith.'

The wind increased in ferocity. I stood transfixed as great sheets of water passed through the incorporeal body of the captain. The three of us were not so lucky, and it wouldn't be long before we'd be drenched again. Without saying another word, we ran to the door and down to the cabin.

'What's a Baobhan Sith?' Cassie said as we got inside and dried ourselves.

Kai draped a towel over her head, rubbing her hair as she spoke.

'The Baobhan Sith are female vampires, particular to Scotland.'

I plopped myself on the smallest sofa and stretched my legs, ready for the sleep I knew was imminent. The thought of encountering another vampire, even one who controlled a Hellhound, held no fear for me.

'Get your friend the ghost captain to plan a route up the coast to Scotland, and wake me when we arrive.'

I didn't hear Kai's reply as my eyes closed, and I was asleep in seconds.

I DIDN'T KNOW what time it was when I woke, but I felt great. Cassie sat opposite me, flicking through her phone.

'You snore like a donkey.'

My teeth were wrapped in grit as I spoke to her. 'No, I don't.'

She put down the phone. 'How do you know what you're like when you're sleeping?'

I twisted my shoulder around and sat up, looking for support from Kai, but she wasn't there.

'I'd know if I snore. I'm far too young for that.'

'Yes, but you do have a big nose, Sister.'

'Just like you then, Sister.' We peered at each other in silence for thirty seconds before bursting out in laughter. My ribs ached, and I was glad to see her happy. And then I glanced at her arm. 'How is your injury?'

Cassie grinned at me. 'It's fine now. While you were snoring, Kai spoke to the captain and he gave her some ghostly ointment which made me all better.'

'Ghostly ointment?' I didn't like the sound of that.

'Yeah, some cream from the bottom of a sunken ship they've had for centuries. Apparently, there are all sorts of cool things on board the captain and his crew have gathered during their travels.'

I wasn't keen on supernatural medicine being used on my sister, but considering what was supposedly inside the both of us, I suppose it didn't really matter.

'Where's Kai?' I said.

'I've got you something to eat,' she said as she came down the stairs. 'It's only bread and cheese, I'm afraid, but it's the best we can do at the moment.'

I took the plate from her. 'Has this been on board the ghost ship for centuries as well?'

Cassie bit at hers. 'It's okay. I've had a lot worse over the years.'

I put mine down and spoke to Kai. 'When do we get to the Hellhound?'

She rubbed at her chin. 'Ah, well, it's going to take a bit longer than I first thought. The captain informs me we have to take a bit of a detour first.'

Cassie dribbled cheese on to the floor. 'A detour to where?'

Kai held out her hands. 'It won't be long, just a little trip to deliver some passengers to their destination.'

She was delaying the news. 'Where are we going, Kai?'

The Warwitch sat down and peered at us both.

'We're going to Purgatory, girls.'

9 PURGATORY

'Purgatory? Why are we going there?'

Kai shifted in her seat. 'Now, Alice, don't worry, it will only be a short detour, and then we'll be back on track to find your mother.'

Cassie didn't seem too concerned as she ate her cheese.

'I thought we'd already been there to find that demon, Bartos?'

I sat back down and nibbled on the food Kai had brought us as the Warwitch answered Cassie's question.

'No, Limbo and Purgatory are two different places. Limbo is where souls go before the decision is made regarding their journey to Heaven or Hell. Purgatory is where souls are purified of their sin.'

Cassie licked her lips. 'So, after death, it's Purgatory, Limbo, then Heaven or Hell?'

'Not quite,' Kai said. 'Purgatory is only for those who need purification. Those who don't need that go to Limbo, while some go straight to Heaven or Hell, dependent upon their earthly actions. And others linger after death in one of the ghostly or shadow realms.'

'This sounds very complicated,' Cassie said. 'I went to a few schools riddled with confusing cliques, but even they seem better than what you've said.'

My brain had woken up, and even though I was mildly irritated we'd been delayed on finding our mother, I was fascinated by Kai's words.

'When you say Purgatory is for purification of sin, who decides on what constitutes sin?' I asked her the question even though I'd already guessed what the answer would be.

Kai held up her hands. 'That's for a higher power than me to decide.'

Cassie sat cross-legged on the sofa. 'Plenty of adults have called me a sinner over the years, so does that mean I'll end up in Purgatory?'

'You're going to be there soon anyway, Sister, by the sound of it.'

She laughed at me. 'At least I'll have you to keep me company.'

Kai didn't join in with our frivolity. 'Don't be confused by what sections of humanity deem to be sinful. The decision comes from the Divine and is more to do with what harm we do to others than having lifestyles some may find offensive.'

'I've been called a lot worse than offensive in my sixteen years, Kai,' Cassie said.

I threw a piece of bread at my sister. 'You probably deserved a few of those.'

Cassie grinned at me and shook her head. 'So, if some religious book tells me I'm a sinner for wanting to kiss a girl, that won't get me into Purgatory?'

'Who do you think wrote those religious books?' Kai said.

'God?' Cassie replied.

Kai stared at my sister. 'No, of course not. The Creator's Divine messages are not communicated through words or texts. All the books claiming to be the Word of God are nothing but the words of men.' She turned from Cassie to me. 'As long as you live your lives in kindness and generosity, you have no fear of finding Purgatory.'

'Apart from now,' I said.

'Yes,' Kai replied.

I stood and flexed my damaged fingers, wondering why I hadn't got any of the magic cream Cassie had for her burns.

'So why is the *Flying Dutchman* heading to Purgatory?'

Before she could reply, a large wailing sound blew the dust from the ceiling. Cassie coughed as she waved her hands in front of her eyes.

'What's that?'

Kai fiddled with the edge of the sofa. 'I assume we've reached our destination. It's probably best we stay down here while the captain goes about his business.'

'Sod that,' I said before running above deck.

Everywhere was calm when I got there, peering into a clear blue sky as Cassie bumped into me. Kai slunk up the steps as we strode to the front, where the captain and his crew peered over the edge. An eerie silence settled over me and a chill ran down my spine. The ghostly captain raised his bony hand over the side while his shipmates stood unmoving.

I whispered to Kai. 'Do you know what's happening?'

She nodded. 'Captain van der Decken has brought the *Flying Dutchman* to the Taiwan Strait. Do you know where that is?'

A sudden image of Akemi in the university bar flashed across my eyes.

'Is it the sea between China and Taiwan?'

'It is. Somewhere below us is the USS *Defiant* and the remains of its three hundred crew.'

I didn't know what else to say, so I stood there in silence, watching as the air moved around us. Then a tremendous rumbling sound came from below, and I gazed down at the sea rising up the side of the *Dutchman*. The water bubbled, and everywhere smelt of burning.

'Is he going to raise the ship?' Cassie said.

'Watch,' Kai said.

So we did. The water stopped moving and shadows rose to the surface, and then broke through. It wasn't the USS *Defiant* that came, but the uniformed bodies of men and women. Three or four at first, but then many more: dozens and dozens until there must have been more than a hundred.

I pressed one hand against my heart and held on to Cassie with the other, my mouth wide open as the dead floated across the sea and on to the *Flying Dutchman*. Then, as I struggled to breathe, they all dropped towards the deck. They disappeared before hitting the ship.

'What happened?' I said.

Kai turned to me. 'What you saw wasn't the bodies of those unfortunate people, but their souls. It's Captain van der Decken's responsibility to transport them to Purgatory for purification.'

Cassie let go of me, glaring at the captain with fire in her eyes.

'What sins will they have committed?'

Kai shrugged. 'I can't answer that, Cassie. It might be something as simple as a petty theft, or perhaps a major indiscretion. Only the Purifiers of Purgatory will know what sins those souls carry with them.'

My sister pulled away from us and strode to the captain.

'What right do you have to pass judgement on anyone?'

I ran to her side, supporting Cassie in her defiance, equally troubled by what I'd witnessed. Captain van der Decken's eyes were nothing but fiery balls of red, his lips unmoving. With his head pointed at us, it was impossible to know if he even recognised our presence.

Kai pulled us both away. 'Don't blame the captain; he's only doing what he has to. His job is to transport the souls to Purgatory. He doesn't choose or judge them.'

'Yes, you said. It's up to these Purifiers.'

The words crawled over my lips. Before I could say anything else, the ship lurched forward and the crew vanished from the deck. Captain van der Decken continued to look in our direction before he turned away and disappeared.

'He and the crew have gone to get the souls ready and plot our journey.' Kai took hold of Cassie and my hands. 'Whatever you do in Purgatory, don't get off this boat.' She couldn't hide the fear in her eyes. 'No matter what you see or hear, you have to stay here. Do you understand?' We both nodded. 'It's probably best if we all go back below deck.'

'No.' Defiance seeped out of Cassie. 'I want to see where this journey takes us.' She smiled at me. 'Wherever it is, it can't be worse than Hell, right? And we know we're going there.'

I put my hand on her shoulder. 'Whatever happens, we stay together, Sister.'

Before we could do anything else, a thick mist appeared from nowhere and covered the whole of the ship.

'Crap,' Cassie said as we held hands.

'Don't move,' I said. 'Kai, are you there?'

'Yes, Alice. I'm near the entrance which goes below the deck. Are you two okay?'

'We're fine.' Even though my heart was thumping at a hundred beats a minute. 'Do you know what this is?'

'I'd guess it's part of the route to Purgatory, and we've now left the Earthly realm. It shouldn't last long.'

She wasn't wrong. The mist clung to my face and smelt of a graveyard, but disappeared after a few minutes. What surrounded us now was a different environment: the sea was pitch black, the sky nothing but grey. Grim moving shadows twisted through the grey, but didn't approach the ship.

The captain and his crew reappeared to guide the vessel to a bleak, desolate shore. There was no sand or stone there, but something which moved when the *Flying Dutchman* reached it. Large shapes wriggled below the dark water as the souls from the USS *Defiant* floated off the ship towards a mountain onshore.

I placed my hands on the side of the ship. 'Is this Purgatory?'

'Yes, Alice. Remember what I said. Don't leave this spot, no matter what.'

Cassie pointed at the mountain. 'There are holes in it, like a Swiss cheese.'

She was right, and the dead floated towards those holes. Or so it seemed at first, until I realised the mountain had somehow moved closer to us. Now I could see what was happening to the crew of the USS *Defiant* as they entered those cuts into the earth rising in front of us. Their screams made me cover my ears, but I could still hear everything.

'What's happening, Kai?' Cassie said.

'In each opening, sinners are tormented by demons and by fire. Each of the seven deadly sins - avarice, envy, sloth, pride, anger, lust, and gluttony - has its region of Purgatory and its appropriate tortures.'

I turned away from the sight. 'Can we go now?'

'I told you to stay below deck, Alice.'

My body ached as I turned to leave, only stopped by Cassie's hand on my arm.

'Did you hear that?'

'What?' Her eyes were wide and nervous. 'What was it, Cassie?'

She gripped on to me. 'Listen, Alice. She's calling our names.'

And then I heard it.

Alice. Cassie. Please help me.

It was more of an echo than a voice, a vibration inside my head and not my ears.

Alice. Cassie. Please help me.

I gazed towards the mountain, seeing the new souls transported there tortured and torn apart.

'Where is it coming from?'

Kai grabbed my elbow. 'We must go, girls.'

I twisted out of her grip. 'Can't you hear that, Kai?'

Alice. Cassie. Please help me.

'All I hear are the screams of Purgatory, Alice. Now let's go down below until this journey is over.'

'No.' I gazed across the writhing beach that wasn't sand. 'I can see where it's coming from.'

Cassie pointed to the closest opening in the mountain. 'So can I.'

Alice. Cassie. Please help me. Save me, my children.

'Mother!' Cassie and I said together.

Then we ran as one, jumping over the side of the ship with no thought of what would happen when we landed. My feet hit something soft and I rolled forward, watching

Cassie as she did the same. What was beneath me was unnatural, slimy and wet, but I didn't care as I pushed myself up.

But I didn't move. A grey hand held on to my leg: a grey hand coming out of the ground.

'It's human flesh,' Cassie said near me as two hands grabbed her. 'It's a beach of skin and bone.'

I kicked at the fingers holding me, hitting my leg, but I ignored the pain as the thing let me go. Then I ran to Cassie and pulled her away from that inhuman grip. The ground writhed and wriggled beneath us as we sprinted forward towards the words calling to us.

Alice. Cassie. Please help me. Save me, my children.

'Lucy must have put Mother here,' I said.

'We'd never have known if it wasn't for the *Dutchman.*'

Fingers popped out of the ground like roots of a tree, springing up with long nails at the end, grasping for us. We dodged all of them and reached the bottom of the mountain, finding rocks which we jumped on. We gazed up to the spot where our mother must have been.

I didn't look back, only up. 'How do we get there?'

'There are indents in the mountain.' Cassie pointed at the gaps I'd missed. 'Are you good at climbing?'

'I went on an indoor climbing wall every weekend before going to university.'

She shook her head. 'I guess that will have to do, but stay close to me.' She put her hand on the mountain. 'God knows what might come out of this if the ground is anything to go by.'

She put her hands and feet into the first gaps and started to climb. I took the ones next to her and followed, ignoring the screams coming from all around us. A sulphuric smoke burnt in the air as my nails dug into our climb.

'Will the ship wait for us?' I said.

'Let's get our mother first, Alice, then we can deal with what comes next.'

She was right, but I still thought of what would happen if the *Dutchman* abandoned us in Purgatory. I kept that thought in my mind to distract me from the sights around us as we climbed. Each opening contained one crew member from the USS *Defiant* surrounded by ghoulish creatures clawing at them or poking them with flaming spears.

The air smelt of burning flesh and the screams kept getting louder. But I could still hear her in my head.

Alice. Cassie. Please help me. Save me, my children.

'She's just above us, Alice.'

We paused for one second before I climbed into the opening with Cassie, fearful of what I'd find.

But it was empty.

'What?' I said.

Cassie was about to reply when four creatures came out of the walls: bald, emaciated, humanoid individuals with decaying hide stretched tight over their bones. They had sharp carnivorous teeth and sunken eyes that burned as if they were hot coals.

Then they all spoke together.

Alice. Cassie. Please help me. Save me, my children.

Invisible fingers clutched at my heart as I noticed the tear in Cassie's eye before she wiped it away.

'What have you done with our mother?'

The creatures cackled in unison, a horrible sound that pricked the hairs on the back of my neck. It was a terrible noise, but what came next was worse.

They sang.

Mary Arcane, Mary Arcane, abandoned her children, and she's to blame.

Mary Arcane, Mary Arcane, abandoned her children, and she's to blame.

Mary Arcane, Mary Arcane, abandoned her children, and she's to blame.

They inched towards us with their great claws pointed at our heads. And still, they sang that song.

Mary Arcane, Mary Arcane, abandoned her children, and she's to blame.

I glanced at Alice as the beasts pounced.

Two landed on me, grasping at my face as I kicked at the first one. Its frame was weedy, and it snapped in half and fell away. But the other one gripped my throat, the nails drawing blood from me as I struggled to breathe.

The creature pushed its face into mine.

We hunt the Children of the Arcane because your death will free us from this place.

Whatever reason it wanted to speak to me, it was its undoing. I thrust my hand into the jaw, which crumbled like dust as I hit it. The rest of the creature followed suit, collapsing into bone all over me. Parts of it got into my mouth and nose. I coughed out as much as I could as I stood.

Cassie was opposite me, crushing a head between her fingers.

'You took your time, Sister.'

I brushed the dead from my clothes. 'Did they talk to you?'

She laughed. 'No. I'm not sure they could say much, apart from pretending to be our mother and singing that terrible song. Did they speak to you?'

'One of them did.'

'What did it say?'

'"We hunt the Children of the Arcane because your death will free us from this place".'

Cassie stepped towards me. 'What's that supposed to mean?'

I shrugged. 'I have no idea.' I kept on wiping the bits from me before stopping. 'What's that noise?' It wasn't the screams of the tortured but something else: an inhuman wail that made me scratch at my ears.

Cassie moved to the edge of the opening and looked out. 'Oh, crap.'

I joined her and saw what she meant: hundreds of those creatures were crawling up the mountain towards us.

They kept on howling as a vast shadow engulfed us.

10 HOUNDS OF LOVE

When my vision returned, daylight was cascading through a window and I lay on a sofa. There were no ghouls anywhere and the mountain had disappeared. Next to me was a bowl of water, a towel, toothpaste and toothbrush, plus a cheese sandwich from Marks and Spencer. I put a hand to my neck, imagining I'd finally woken up from my week-old nightmare and was back in my flat in Middlesbrough, only to find the cut where the creature had attacked me.

'Get cleaned up, have some grub, and then we're off.' Bits of steak and onion dripped from Cassie's lips, grease sticking to her teeth. The smell made me queasy. I wiped the confusion from my eyes.

'What happened? The last thing I remember is those ghouls coming for us in Purgatory.'

My sister grinned at me as food dripped from her lips.

'I saved you, of course. How many times have I done that now?'

A long ache rippled through all of me as I waved a hand at her.

'I'm not counting. And I don't believe you anyway. There were hundreds of those things crawling towards us, and even you're not that good.'

She puffed out her cheeks. 'Well, that's the thanks I get from my own sister.'

My head throbbed and I needed that food. 'Stop messing around, Cassie.'

She grinned at me. 'Okay, but only because it's you. Kai told me all the gory details while you slept. And you snored again.'

'I swear to God, Cassie, I'm going to punch your face in any second now.'

Cassie laughed and stuck her tongue out at me, which was somewhat alarming, seeing her acting like a typical teenager and not the confident monster slayer I'd got used to the last few days.

'Well, we owe our lives to the good captain of this vessel. Apparently, one of the unwritten rules of the *Flying Dutchman* is that anyone, or thing, that comes on to this ship is under his protection, no matter what. So it was he who rescued us from the Purifiers of Purgatory and brought us back here.' She picked something from the back of her mouth and dropped it to the floor. 'Now brush your teeth before anything else. I can smell your bed breath from here.'

I ignored the jab. 'I prefer a shower first thing in the morning.'

Cassie grinned. 'Well, good luck with that on this dump. I suppose we could get the ghosts to pour buckets of water over you.'

The insides of my mouth felt as if something large and hairy had crawled inside it overnight and died there. I grabbed the toothbrush and paste.

'Where are we?'

She finished one sandwich and started on another.

'We're in the port of Leith, close to Edinburgh. Kai went into town for supplies.'

My geography of Scotland wasn't great, but I was sure Edinburgh wasn't where we needed to be.

'I thought we were going to the Highlands?'

Cassie slurped on a coffee and the smell of the caffeine snapped me awake.

'Not anymore. It seems our vampire and her Hellhound have moved into the city.'

I threw cold water over my face, my skin blistering with the chill. I cleaned my teeth and felt better.

'Don't the natives of Leith think it's strange that a centuries-old ship is looking over it?'

'They can't see the ghost ship.' Kai came into the cabin. 'I went to shore using one of their rowing boats.' She was a man again. 'The extra muscle made it less of a chore.'

I dribbled dirty water into the bowl and took some of Cassie's coffee to remove the taste from my mouth.

'How come we ended up in Edinburgh?'

Kai sat opposite me. 'I contacted Vika while you slept, and she gave me directions for here.'

I removed the plastic from the cheese sandwiches. 'How did you get in touch?'

'Through social media. She's an Instagram Influencer.'

I nearly spat the sandwich all over her. 'What?'

'She got sick of the Scottish Highlands, said it was terrible for her skin and moved to some posh place here. She loves social media, though I don't know who or what she's influencing. We'll ask her tonight since we have invites to her latest fancy-dress bash.' I didn't know what to say, so I let her continue as I finished the food. 'We have to be careful in the city as your mugs are in the media.'

The food nearly got stuck in my throat. 'We're in the media?'

Kai nodded. 'I'm afraid so. The police are looking for you in particular, Alice, since it was your flat they traced a deadly viral outbreak too.'

'They're claiming the magical zombie attack as a virus?'

'Well, they could hardly broadcast the truth, could they?' Kai said.

I tried not to think of the terrible deaths of my neighbours.

'It was all to get at you, Cassie. You've pissed off some powerful people, it seems.'

She chewed on her food. 'That's the story of my life, Sis.'

'As long as you're careful in the city, we should be okay.' Kai said. 'So you best get ready for the party.'

'At least we can go as pirates,' Cassie said. 'Perhaps wear hats or scarves over our faces.'

I dropped the empty plastic on to the table. 'When does this party start?'

'From six o'clock,' Kai said.

I checked the time on my phone. I'd slept through the night, and it was nearly midday. Fighting the supernatural must have been good for my insomnia.

'So what do we do before then?'

An irritating itch circled my brain. I sent a quick text to Medusa to check up on her, assuming she'd been worried sick about me.

'We come up with a plan,' Cassie said.

Kai made her way out of the cabin. 'I'll return later. I need to speak to the captain.' As she left, Cassie and I stared at our respective phones.

'At least this threat of a world war has relegated us to the outer edges of the news cycle.'

It didn't make me feel any better as I searched for my name online. Every piece I found, and there were more than half a dozen, used those same photos. They classed us as Persons of Interest in the murder of Jack Chase, aged twenty and from Newcastle. There was no mention of an eyewitness or his family. But there was a link to my address and what happened with my neighbours. A statement from an Artemis spokesperson said they were very concerned for me and urged me to hand myself in to the authorities. They'd branded Cassie as a runaway of no fixed abode. There was a hint of previous involvement with the police.

I put the phone down and focused on her.

'What's this about you having a juvenile record?'

She licked a stray onion from the corner of her lips and into her mouth.

'Don't all teenagers get into trouble with the authorities?'

'Not me.'

'Well, you are now.'

I resisted the urge to say it was all because of her, remembering she was the one who'd saved me from Chase, the twenty-year-old Geordie werewolf.

'Do you want to talk about it?'

Cassie shrugged. 'I believe we've got more important things to worry about.'

She showed me her phone and the headline about peace talks in London and Washington, with Prime Minister Howard acting as a moderator between the Americans and the Chinese. Once again, I thought of Akemi. And then I remembered those poor souls from the USS *Defiant* and what happened to them in Purgatory.

'Do you think those people from the ship will get out of Purgatory?'

'I guess so, at some point. From what Kai said, most end up in one place or the other eventually.'

'Heaven or Hell?' I said.

'It looks that way.' She grinned at me. 'Are you still an atheist, Alice?'

I threw a small piece of bread at her head. 'What do you think?'

'I think the world is likely to come to a nuclear end, all because of the archangels, and they won't let these peace talks happen.'

Maybe she was right. 'Do you remember the girl I was with in the park when we first met?'

'When I saved you from the werewolf?'

'Yes, okay. Well, that girl was Akemi. She told me she was working for Taiwan's secret nuclear programme, but I thought she was joking. With everything that's happening now between China and the US, maybe she wasn't.'

'Do you believe that?'

I didn't know what I believed anymore. Apart from knowing I had to find Mary Arcane.

'Well, we can't do anything about it. We have to concentrate on getting to Hell and finding our mother. If we see Lucy on the way, we can ask her about it.'

Cassie put her phone away. 'Okay, we need to decide what we'll say to this vamp when we get to the party.'

She was right. 'Forewarned is forearmed,' I said as I searched for Vika Vistala on Instagram. She was easy to find, with many photos of her: flame-red hair, piercing green eyes and sculpted cheekbones. Vampires may not have had reflections, or Dracula didn't, but this one was photogenic. She looked like a supermodel. I scanned a few comments about her. 'None of these articles mention her age, which I suppose they wouldn't if she's a vampire.'

'Every woman I've met over twenty has lied about their age, and I've never understood why.' Cassie stared at the rack of skulls at the back of the cabin as she spoke.

I read more. 'Vika states she's a vampire on her profile and sells merchandise with it on. Thousands of people buy this stuff: shirts, posters, socks, scarves, all kinds of junk. She even has her face printed on to mugs.'

Cassie snorted laughter. 'They're mugs, all right.' She looked at the screen. 'There's glorious sunshine in most of these photos.'

I glanced through them. 'So?'

'Vampires can't go out in the daylight.'

I considered what she said, recalling what I'd read in *Dracula*.

'According to Bram Stoker's book, the sun was not fatal to Dracula, as sunlight doesn't burn and destroy him upon contact, though most of his abilities cease.' Cassie narrowed her eyes at me. 'You've met vampires before. Were any of those encounters during the day?'

She nodded. 'Some, but they were inside. Is there any mention of this Hellhound?'

I couldn't see any. 'Nope, but she has ten cats.'

Cassie placed her hands behind her head and settled in for the afternoon.

'Great. I love cats. What's the plan when we get there?'

'I have no idea. Maybe she'll let us borrow the beast.' It seemed unlikely, but we could only ask.

We spent the rest of the time scanning websites. Medusa gave me an update on a blind woman she was flirting with online. I'd never flirted with anyone in my life, but I was pleased for her. I tried not to think about archangels, Hell, or the possibility of the world burning from a nuclear war.

At five o'clock, Kai returned carrying two large straw hats. She threw one at each of us.

'It's time to go, girls. Pull these low over your heads as part of your disguise.'

'Can vampires move around in the daylight?'

Kai peered at my sister. 'They lose most of their abilities under the sun, but it won't harm them if they've fed.'

'Fed?' I said.

'As long as they've drunk enough human blood, their immune system can fend off the destruction sunlight would do to them if they were weak.'

A shiver ran down my spine as I thought of Bella wiping blood from her lips.

'And if they haven't fed?'

Kai looked at me. 'I once watched a group of vampires burst into flame when humans dragged them into the sun. It was a horrific sight.' She rubbed at her nose. 'And the smell was terrible.'

Cassie put the hat on. 'Can we get something to eat on the way? I'm starving.'

'There'll be food at the party. Vika is looking forward to meeting you both.'

As we made our way on to the deck, I still didn't know how we'd convince her to lend us the Hellhound. The captain and his crew waited there like a spectral welcoming committee. I clutched the hat in my hand and strode towards him.

'Thank you for rescuing us twice and bringing us to Scotland.' His face was emotionless, the lines etched over his yellow skin unmoving. But at least the fiery red eyes had been replaced by a swirling yellow hue, which was quite calming. 'And thank you for providing us with fresh clothes.' We were ready to get into the small boat and head into Leith, but I had one last thing to say to this man who'd saved us. 'I'm going to Hell to save my mother, but if I come across God in my travels, I'll make sure they release all of you from this curse.' There was a slight flicker in his eye as I turned and climbed down the rope.

'It looks like we're rowing.'

Cassie was at the far end of the boat, Kai, back in her female form, sitting between us. I don't think either of us had rowed a boat before, so it was a struggle to get the oars through the water in a straight line. As I glanced over my shoulder, the *Flying Dutchman* vanished into the mist, the captain's shining yellow eyes the last thing I saw as we set our sights on Leith.

The wind and the sun caressed my face as we headed to the quayside. The exercise made my arms ache, but in a good way, my body enjoying the work. Kai had her phone in her hand as the boat rocked up to the concrete.

'I'll order a taxi.'

We were off to see a vampire about a dog.

We came through Leith Docks, our faces hidden to the sun and prying eyes. The air smelt of the sea as Kai moored the boat.

'You're in good company taking this journey into Scotland, girls. Mary Queen of Scots travelled the same route to begin her reign of this wild and wonderful place.'

'And look how well that ended for her,' Cassie said.

I climbed out of the boat. 'It sounds like you're speaking as someone who was there, Kai.'

She laughed and shook her head. 'I'm not that old, Alice.' She tied the boat to the quayside. 'But I do know my history, and poor Mary was betrayed by many she thought loyal to her.'

'Her cousin signed Mary's death warrant.' I knew that from my studies.

Cassie put her hand on my shoulder. 'Maybe family are not to be trusted after all.'

I ignored her jab. 'Are we going to leave the boat here?' I had visions of us having to abandon the city in a hurry and return to the ghost ship.

'I don't think we need to worry about that,' Cassie said as our lift disappeared into nothingness. It coincided with our taxi arriving.

Kai waved at the driver, but spoke to us. 'Are you ready?'

I nodded. 'How well do you know this vampire?'

The Warwitch narrowed her eyes. 'We went to school together.'

A long, rasping laugh burst from Cassie. 'That must have been interesting for your teachers.'

'I'll tell you all about it someday, but it wasn't like being at Hogwarts, that's for sure. But let's take the taxi, and you can imagine what it was like on the way to Vika's place.'

As she gave the driver the directions to Vika Vistala's home, we got into the back with our hats pulled down as far as they'd go so we could still see the city.

'It's a long time since we've had pirates coming into town through the docks,' the driver said as he drove off. Kai gave him a knowing grin as Cassie and I kept quiet and surveyed our surroundings as we headed away. We rode past newly built residential dwellings, shops, leisure facilities, bars and restaurants, and I realised it was my first visit to Scotland.

The car travelled from Leith Docks and into the heart of Edinburgh, with a surprising amount of green along the way, including the Royal Botanic Garden. I spotted a sign for Edinburgh Zoo, but we went in the other direction.

It took about ten minutes to get there, and when we did, I realised why Vika Vistala had moved from the wilds of the Scottish Highlands and into the nation's capital: it wasn't a Disney castle, but not far off. Even Cassie was impressed.

'Wow!' A hive of bees could have nestled in her open

mouth. We stumbled from the car, staring at the building in admiration. Having lived in many places over the years, I'd never been one to get too attached to concrete and houses, but this was somewhere I could have settled in. Sculptured gardens surrounded the castle, bushes cut into the shapes of mythical beasts, or what I'd once thought was mythical: tiny dragons, a centaur, winged horses, and, as we strode to the entrance, clumps of colourful flowers looking like the harpies we'd fought in Limbo.

Butterflies hovered around as we walked up the steps. Kai was about to knock on the door when it opened. A woman dressed as a 1920s flapper greeted us with open arms.

'Welcome to the home of Vika Vistala.' She gazed at Cassie and me as we removed our hats. 'You must be the twins she's been speaking about so much.' She leant forward. 'I love your pirate costumes, and you even smell of the sea.' I couldn't tell if it was an insult or not.

We followed her inside, the place bouncing with noise: people talking and loud electronic dance music playing somewhere above. There were hallways on both sides, a party buzz coming from them, while ahead was an aroma of cooked food floating from the kitchen.

'Do you know where Vika is?' Kai said to the woman.

She shook her head. 'The last time I saw her, she was in the Great Hall.' She pointed to our left. 'But she's such a social butterfly she could be anywhere. This is the ground floor. There are also upper and lower floors, the stairs to which are past the dining room on your right. There's a lift further on as well.' She gazed at Kai as she spoke before heading into the kitchen and leaving us to our own devices.

I nodded left. 'We might as well start in the Great Hall.'

From the outside, the castle may have looked as if built five hundred years ago, but the insides had undergone several modern makeovers. The floor was fresh wood and fluffy carpets, with bare walls apart from the odd paintings I assumed were reproductions of Picassos and Van Goghs and not the originals. The ceiling contained no antique chandeliers, but contemporary lighting.

As we approached, a crowd left the Great Hall, dressed as Victorian dandies, scary clowns, muscular men and vivacious women looking like ancient Romans or Greeks, a tall woman in tennis gear, and two rotund blokes as Teletubbies. It was a strange mixture, and they all ignored us as we entered the room.

Servants handed out drinks while placing trays of food on tables around the edges of the room. Cassie headed for the grub, and I followed. She grabbed a chicken leg and pulled at it with her teeth as if she hadn't eaten in a week. I picked a cucumber sandwich and nibbled at it, suddenly too nervous to stop the grumbling in my stomach.

'There are quite a few celebs here,' Cassie said while eating.

I looked across the crowd, seeing nobody I recognised amongst all the fancy clothes.

'Am I supposed to know some of these people?'

Cassie pointed to where the biggest group was. 'See them over there?' I nodded. 'The tall woman looking like Michelle Obama is one of the biggest stars on TikTok. The good-looking bloke next to her is an Instagram fashion model, and the two identical blonde girls with them are YouTube singing sensations.' She peered at me with curious eyes. 'You must have lived like a social media hermit before going to university.'

'Okay.' I lost interest in them and focused on another

group. 'What about the pasty-faced girl who makes a ghost look healthy or the bloke with teeth down to his chin? Then there's the green-skinned woman, plus the ten-foot-tall guy. Are they famous as well?'

Cassie shrugged. 'It's a fancy dress party, Alice; what do you expect?'

Kai stepped between us. 'Vika is popular in the supernatural world as well as the human one.'

Cassie spat a piece of chicken on to the floor. 'So there are monsters here with us as well?'

Kai waved a finger at her. 'You have to stop using terms like that, Cassie. I thought you'd learnt by now not to discriminate against those of supernatural origin. Not all of us are beasts, you know.'

I could see my sister was ready to argue the point when a roar erupted from the middle of the hall. We finished eating and strolled towards it. As the cowboys and cowgirls, robots and space people separated, we gazed upon the Queen in her throne: Vika Vistala sat in an ornate chair, acolytes fawning at her feet. In the flesh, the vampire's hair was redder than an exploding sun, her lips more luscious and purple than the glossiest plum, and when her eyes found us, the green shimmered brighter than the freshest cut grass. There was no sign of her Hellhound, the creature we'd gone there for and who we still had little idea of how to get.

Kai pushed her way through the crowd, and we followed.

The music grew into a crescendo, partygoers bouncing around the room like planets orbiting their sun. I pulled on Kai's arm.

'What are we going to say to her about the Hellhound?'

Cassie and I had spent all afternoon discussing it and still had no solution.

'I'll sweet talk her,' Kai said, and I wondered if there was something about the two of them she hadn't mentioned. Was the comment about them going to school together true?

As I checked the room, it seemed as if there were more supernatural attendees than humans. A sudden pain gripped my heart as I worried if Kai had performed a long confidence trick to get us there surrounded by those who wanted to do us harm. What if there were no humans present and every living thing in the building was a supernatural creature? Was it a trap after all?

I shook the stupidity of it from my head. Kai had done nothing but help us since that first meeting in Whitby and had saved our lives at least once. Perhaps the strange-smelling smoke lingering in the air was confusing my senses. I waved a hand around my head as we moved towards the centre of attention.

As we got closer, four pure white cats flitted around Vika's seat, and every one of them had the same piercing green eyes as their owner.

'How nice it is to see you again, my old friend.' Authority and affection oozed from her voice, her lips glistening as we stood before her.

Kai surprised me and bowed. 'It's always a pleasure, Vika.'

'But this time, your visit is purely business.' Her gaze cut through me as if green rays had sunk beneath my eyes and burrowed deep into the rest of my body.

'Can we talk in private?' It was a gentle request, full of deference. The vampire pondered the question as the music and frivolity increased. What would we do if we couldn't use her Hellhound?

'Of course, of course. I need something to eat anyway.'

Cassie nibbled on a piece of cheese she must have taken earlier. 'There's plenty of food in here.'

The vampire queen scrutinised my sister as if she was the first course of the evening.

'Oh no, that's only for the guests. What I need is in the next room.'

Vika stepped from her seat, her long, sinewy legs moving against the skin-tight purple dress she wore. Everyone only had eyes for her as she strode down and we shifted out of the way. Her arm glanced against mine as she went, an exotic scent of musk confusing my senses. The whole of the room parted for her as she left, we three following like servants glued to their mistress. What was it about vampires that made them so magnetic? This was the third one I'd met, and each time it was unnerving how my mind lapsed into a mental fog.

We exited the Great Hall and strode towards the stairs. Vika stepped ahead, turning to glance at Cassie and me.

'I've been following you girls in the media; werewolves are such dirty creatures.' We said nothing. Partygoers slid out of the way at her approach.

'I'm surprised you moved from the serenity of nature and into the city,' Kai said to her friend.

Vika appeared to glide across the carpet, her feet hidden behind that flowing dress. Her laugh was light, like leaves fluttering on a breeze.

'I think you've been inside your Impossible Palace for too long, Kai, if you believe nature is anything but wild and untamed. I came here for a bit of peace, but I've had to deal with several unforeseen problems.'

A door opposite opened without anyone touching it. She stepped inside, and we followed her in, the door closing behind us on its own. The room was windowless, empty apart from several bookshelves brimming with volumes, and black and white photographs covering the walls. I went to the books, expecting them to be dusty first editions or ancient tomes hundreds of years old. Instead, they were all paperbacks, every shelf crammed with popular fiction, from crime to erotica and romance.

I was reaching for a Raymond Chandler I'd never heard of when Cassie shouted behind me.

'Damn! Come and look at this, Alice.'

I went to her as she peered at one section of the photo-filled wall, wondering if she'd seen some pointless internet celebrity again. She hadn't, and it was a lot stranger than that.

Vika appeared at our sides like a ninja. 'Do you like my collection?'

It was hard to focus on the photos, my eyes unsure which image to look at. The people in each one moved as if they were in a small video clip: there was a man in a top hat stroking a small dog, a young girl playing with a peculiar looking cat, a woman eating ice cream, a group of boys kicking a football around a desolate landscape, and so many others. I turned away before the sights hurt my eyes.

'I'm surprised you kept them all,' Kai said.

I twisted my head to see Vika reply to her. 'I couldn't leave them in that place, old friend. I took them into the highlands with me, but I had to pack them away in a long box, a terrible place for them to be; I had no choice. Now, here, they can breathe again.'

'What are they?' I said.

Kai took my hand and led me to a sofa I hadn't noticed when we came in.

'What you see on the walls are not photographs, but

living lanterns: images snapped from life, and then contained in a frame.' She glanced at Vika. 'I didn't think I'd see them again.'

Cassie sat next to me. 'Those are real people in the photos?'

'Yes,' Vika said. 'Cursed to spend all eternity trapped where they are.'

Kai let go of me. 'Are the worse ones here?'

The vampire shook her head. 'No. I keep those away from sensitive eyes.'

My body trembled as I stood. 'What do you mean when you say worse ones?'

'Some living lanterns contain things you wouldn't want to see,' Vika said.

'Like what?' Cassie said.

Vika sighed. 'You have to perceive these as trapped souls. Most of these prisoners are unaware of where they are, but some realise, and they can't hide their pain. Gazing upon them can burn your soul.'

The horror of it made my stomach churn. 'Who would do such a thing and why?'

Kai replied. 'We don't know who created them, but I guess some powerful person thought it amusing.'

'Can't anything be done to help the people trapped inside?' I thought of those I'd left behind at the Nexus, in Limbo and Purgatory. And how I'd failed so many times.

Vika took a small bell from a shelf and rang it. 'Their only escape is if we burn the images.'

'Will they die?' I said.

'Of course,' Vika said as she turned her eyes from me and towards the young woman who entered the room. She had a blonde bob and looked not much older than Cassie or me.

My gaze returned to the photos that weren't photos as if some unseen force pulled at my brain. As I fought that temptation, the blonde woman went to Vika and bent her neck towards the vampire. Before I could do anything, our host bit into the skin and drew blood.

12   HOUND DOG

Cassie jumped up to stop the vampire, but Kai pulled her back.

'What she does is her choice, giving her blood to Vika.'

Cassie jerked away from her. 'How do you know that? What if the vampire hypnotised her or forced her to do this?'

Vika finished her meal, and the girl pulled up with a smile. A small trickle of blood lingered on her skin as the vampire wiped at her mouth.

'Sophia, tell the girls why you're here.'

Her finger contained a spot of blood as she spoke. 'I give myself willingly to my Queen.'

I gazed into her eyes, searching for some sign she was under duress or confused, but there was none. Cassie glared at Vika.

'Is this what Instagram Influencers do? They get their followers to sacrifice part of themselves to those they worship?'

Vika appeared unfazed by my sister's stern gaze. 'Isn't that what all of us do to some extent: give parts of ourselves, of our souls, to satisfy some need we have?' She glanced at the blonde woman. 'Sophia could leave here and return to her normal human life. What was it again?'

'I had two jobs,' Sophia said. 'Behind the bar in a pub at night, and as a server in a coffee shop during the day. I needed both to pay the rent on a small flat in the city. The neighbours always had loud parties, and the landlord harassed me all the time.' She smiled at Vika. 'I much prefer it here.'

'They're not your only choices in life,' I said.

Sophia rolled up her sleeves and showed me the bruises on her arm.

'I could go back to my parents.'

I peered at her and didn't know how to help her. Maybe I was wrong to think I needed to.

Kai clapped her hands. 'Okay, shall we talk about the Hellhound? I assume you still have it, Vika?'

'Follow me,' the vampire said.

We stepped out of the room behind her, but Sophia stayed. Vika led us down a long corridor until we hit the intersection of the stairs, where one flight went up and the other down. Vika took us on the descent.

'What problems were you talking about earlier?' Kai said.

We followed the vampire into the bowels of the building for two minutes.

'You'll see,' she said as we reached the bottom. A large door waited there. Vika pushed it open and we stepped inside. I expected a dungeon or a kennel for the Hellhound; instead, it was a bright white room, thinly furnished apart from six wooden poles going from the ground to the ceiling.

Tied to these were men, all dressed in similar suits. It was like a board meeting gone wrong. Every one of them unleashed a volley of obscenities as we entered, most aimed at the vampire. She let them scream and shout until their faces were baked red.

I stared at them. 'What is this?'

Her lips curled as she spoke, purple glistening in the artificial light. 'People call us monsters, but the real ones are humans who prey on their own kind. We have lunatics ready to turn the planet into a nuclear fireball, and then we have parasites like these six.' Her voice rose a little, the green burning inside her eyes.

'What have they done?'

Vika strode across the room and undid the restraints of the man closest to her. I waited for him to lunge forward, but he rubbed his hands and scanned his surroundings. She stepped back from him.

'These six control all the crime in the city: human trafficking, murder, prostitution, child grooming, robbery, fraud, and everything else you can think of. I was shocked to see so much crime on arriving here, assuming the authorities would deal with people like this. I warned these men what would happen if they didn't stop, but do you know what they did?' She turned her back on him and looked at me.

'They laughed at you?'

Her eyes narrowed into near pinpricks. 'They murdered two trafficked women and dumped their bodies at my front door.'

What could I say to that? I watched as the free man moved his head and flexed his shoulders. The temperature changed, heat seeping in from somewhere. The hairs prickled on the back of my neck, my fingers tingling with the difference in the atmosphere. Something else was with us, a presence we couldn't see. A stink of brimstone and sulphur swept across the room as an invisible entity brushed past me.

The man stepped towards Vika. 'And we'll kill many more now because of your interference.'

No sooner had the words left his lips than half of his face was cut to ribbons by unseen claws. He tried to scream, but his flesh fell from his cheek, his muscle and tissue dropping on to the floor.

'Shit!' Cassie grabbed me and pulled us back towards the door. As she did so, the man's head was sheared from his shoulders, hurtling through the air and striking the next bloke in the room as he cringed against the wood. Blood flew, the decapitated body hitting the ground and the stink of burning copper invading my nostrils.

There was no time to speak before the Hellhound struck again, slicing open a man's stomach, guts tumbling out in a heap. He got off a scream before the invisible beast bit through his throat. The creature went through three more captives in quick succession. One was left alive, trembling against the pole, as heads were devoured, disappearing into space where the Hellhound's jaws must have been.

I slumped against the wall, wanting to take my eyes away from the carnage but finding it impossible. Cassie and Kai watched, their faces convulsing in what I could only think was the same horror I felt. As the last survivor wailed, Vika approached him and undid his restraints.

'Go back and tell every member of organised crime in this city they have twenty-four hours to comply with my will, or you'll suffer the same fate as your colleagues.'

He sobbed and shook, piss dripping down his leg and staining the floor. The stink of it made me want to gag. He stumbled from the room and I shivered at the horrors I'd witnessed.

How could we control this beast?

'Can I see this dog?' Cassie was in better command of her emotions than I, facing up to Vika Vistala. The vampire grinned at her through purple lips, and then whistled.

'Show yourself, Scooby.'

As I considered how inappropriate the name was for a Hellhound, it flickered into visibility, the sight of it as shocking as its actions. It was as big as a horse, covered in thick green fur, with saucer-like eyes burning yellow and red. It moved towards me, an aroma of scorched brimstone and sulphur coming from it. The brute stopped two inches from Cassie, its head tilting down at hers. She didn't flinch.

'That's an unusual name for a Hell beast.' Cassie and the creature peered into each other's eyes.

Vika took hold of my hand and led me to Scooby, my shock preventing me from resisting.

'It's a good name for a dog who battles evil, isn't it, Scooby?'

She ruffled the hound's chin before placing my palm on its cheek. It was warm to my fingers and no different from every other mutt I'd touched. The supernatural fire in its eyes diminished, and I could have sworn it smiled at me.

'We want to borrow it,' Cassie said.

My hand continued to battle my instinct to turn and flee, stroking its massive green fuzz. Vika let go of me and stepped away.

'I don't own Scooby. I'm not his mistress and he goes where he wants.'

'So why is he with you?' Kai's voice trembled.

Vika stood in the middle of the room. 'A long time ago, when I wasn't as strong as I am now, Scooby came to my rescue when humans with pitchforks and torches pursued me through hills and woods. He's been by my side ever since.' She stared at the hound as it snuggled against my hand. 'But I believe it's time he found other adventures, and he appears to have made a new friend.'

Scooby moved his head to mine. My heart fluttered against my ribs as his fur pressed into my skin, adrenaline coursing through my veins. A low murmur drifted from his throat towards me.

'Do you think he'll help us find Hell?' Cassie said.

Vika shrugged her shoulders. 'If you help me, I'm sure Scooby will help you.'

'Help you how?' Kai said.

'I require something from you, old friend.'

'And what would that be?'

Vika clasped her hands together. 'I have no faith in humans. They'll soon bring unholy fire down on this world, and if that happens, I need somewhere safe to live.'

'You want the Guardianship of the Impossible Palace.' Kai sounded disappointed. 'You want to take my place there.'

'Why can't she just stay with you?' I didn't understand the situation, confused by what was happening between them.

The vampire puckered her lips and blew out hot air. 'There can be only one curator at a time inside the Impossible Palace. Otherwise, it will destroy the balance, and it will collapse in on itself. There is only ever one permanent Guardian, and it has to be passed on willingly.'

Scooby dropped to the floor and rubbed against my legs. He continued to murmur like a baby. There was an immediate connection between us and I was unwilling to break it, but there was a sudden suspicion the vampire was only using this to force her way into Kai's home. I couldn't let that happen.

'No, it doesn't matter; we'll find another way into Hell.'

'You won't because there are no gates or doorways into Hell. Unless you're Satan, the only way in or out of Hell is with a Hellhound, because they are the doorway.'

My heart sank like a stone as Scooby rolled over my feet.

'I'll do it,' Kai said.

'Let's get a move on, then.' Cassie was raring to go. I moved away from the friendly dog and went to Kai.

'You needn't do this; we can find another solution.' I said it, but didn't believe it. This was the only chance of rescuing our mother.

Kai pulled me aside. 'It's okay, Alice. Perhaps it's time for a change in my life.'

'So, how do we do this?' Cassie said.

The vampire played with the Hellhound's ears. 'Scooby is your transport to Hell, but you also need a key to get inside.'

Why didn't it surprise me there would be another obstacle in our way?

'Do you have this key?'

Vika shook her head. 'I did, but the fairies stole it from me.'

'Fairies?' Cassie and I said together.

'Yes, deceitful and untrustworthy creatures. Two of them snuck into one of my parties pretending to be YouTube stars and stole poor Scooby's earring.'

'Earring?' I didn't know if she was messing with us or not. 'You said it was a key.'

She nodded. 'Scooby's earring is the key to the gates of Hell. You need to retrieve it from the thieves, and then you'll have everything you need.'

'Where do we find these fairy thieves?' Cassie said.

'The entrance to the fairy realm is at the Nelson Monument on Calton Hill. Go there, retrieve the key, and then return here. Scooby will be waiting for you.'

Cassie and I looked at each other, and I assumed she knew we had no choice but to do as the vampire said if we were to find our mother.

As I put the directions into my phone, the party continued in full swing as the music increased. I pulled the hat down over my head, glancing at Cassie as we left the grounds.

Two pirates off to find a key to Hell inside the realm of the fairies.

We strode through the city, avoiding prying eyes and not speaking. When we got to Calton Hill, we went past pubs, hip bistros, smart delis and art galleries. Posh townhouses stood tall amongst the occasional restaurant and hotel.

'We should have brought a picnic,' Cassie said as we paused along the grass to stare over the magnificent view of the city. On one side was the Firth of Forth, on the other Princes Street and Edinburgh Castle.

'Maybe next time,' I said as I dragged her towards the Nelson Monument, a distinctive-looking structure constructed in the shape of a telescope.

She wriggled out of my grip. 'Once we get to the top, then what do we do?'

It was a good question. Vika, the vampire, had been vague on how we'd enter this magical fairy realm.

'You'll know when you see it,' she'd said when I'd asked her about an entrance.

At the monument, Cassie pushed through the door first, using her credit card to pay for our tickets. We ignored the museum and headed up the steps. It was a short walk, then we exited on to the viewing gallery. It was a narrow spot, and I was thankful we were the only people there.

'Can you see a magic door?' Cassie said.

I checked the whole of the platform, ran my hands over the stone, and came up with nothing.

'No. Can you?'

She craned her neck up. 'Perhaps it's up there with that ball.'

On top of the tower was a large ball that was raised and lowered to mark the time. I gritted my teeth and wondered if the vampire Instagram Influencer had sent us on a wild goose chase.

But why?

I was considering that question when bright yellow lights flickered in front of me over the edge of the viewing area. They increased in number, flashing between red and yellow as they twirled before me like a kaleidoscope.

'Look at this, Cassie.'

She turned towards me and gazed at the unusual lights.

'Did the vampire slip drugs into our food?'

I stepped closer to the lights, holding out my hand and feeling the heat coming from the illumination.

'No. I think this is our magical doorway.'

Cassie laughed. 'It's six feet over the edge of this thing. How do you suggest we get in?'

I put one hand on the edge and climbed on to the narrow stone. The wind brushed against my face as I tried to ignore the five hundred foot drop below.

'We'll jump,' I said with more confidence than I possessed.

'Wait,' Cassie said as she reached for me.

But it was too late as I leapt over the edge. For one brief, terrible second, I saw the ground below me. And then it disappeared.

I landed and fell into lush, long grass which smelt of mint. I jumped up to search for Cassie, finding myself surrounded by bushes and trees covered with bright flowering leaves, presenting a cavalcade of rainbow colours and an aroma of high summer. On one side was a sparkling river where the clear water rippled in the slight breeze which caressed my face. On the other side were knots of tall pine trees, their trunks gnarled and twisted into weird shapes which almost looked like faces if I peered at them too long.

I took a deep breath to gather my bearings before realising there was something in the closest tree, dangling from the branches like an ornament on a Christmas tree. Only when it started thrashing around did I recognise what it was and run towards it.

'Get me down from here,' Cassie shouted as I grabbed her legs.

'Okay, okay. Stop moving around, or you'll kick me in the head.' She did as I asked and relaxed a little. I took hold of her and held on tight. 'Can you get loose from the branches?'

'If I could, do you think I'd be stuck like this?' I should have felt sympathy for her frustration, but I couldn't stop myself from laughing. She wriggled her legs in my arms again. 'That's okay. You enjoy yourself while I've got my head in a bunch of stinking leaves.'

She sneezed before I could reply.

'It could have been worse, Cassie. That gateway might have led to anywhere.' I gave it more thought now than I had done when I leapt. 'We could have ended up on the moon, choking our guts up with no air to breathe, or at the bottom of the sea.'

'At least I'd be able to move,' she gasped.

'You can move okay. Just try and wriggle your arms free.' I waited for the next set of angry words, but she went silent and completely still. 'Are you all right, Cassie?'

Her legs tensed in my arms. 'There's something on the branch next to my head.'

I laughed. 'Birds won't hurt you.'

'Do birds have poisonous yellow eyes and teeth bigger than my hands?'

Her legs thrashed in my grasp again until she kicked out and I fell back on to the grass. I hit the ground with a thump as the branches around Cassie vibrated as if they were in a hurricane.

I was jumping up to grab at her again when she fell from the tree and landed at my feet. Her hair was a mess, but apart from that, she seemed fine.

I helped her up. 'What happened?'

She brushed leaves from her clothes and glared at me.

'Something snarled at me, and then ran away. But at least its movement shook me loose so I could get down.' She continued to glare. 'No thanks to you.' She wriggled free from my hand and checked our surroundings. 'Where are we?'

We stood in the middle of a collection of mounds and valleys, which reminded me of the Shire from *Lord of the Rings*.

'I guess this is the place Vika mentioned, the place of the fairies.'

'It's pretty enough, I suppose, but where do we start to find the Hellhound's earring?' She continued scanning the area. 'This place looks pretty big.'

I was considering her question when the answer came to me in the air.

'Can you hear that noise?'

Cassie twisted her head as if searching for a set of speakers above us, then twitched her nose like a dog on a hunt.

'It sounds like someone playing the drums.'

'We might as well head for that then.'

The music came from beyond the river, so we set off that way. We strode together, enjoying the idyllic scenery and the aroma of nature. It seemed to me to be the first time in an age I'd relaxed.

'It's beautiful here,' Cassie said. 'I suppose this is a fairy dell or glade.'

I laughed as a smell as sweet as honey slipped into my head.

'You did learn something in school, then?'

She shook her head. 'I'll have you know, Sister of Mine, I'm quite knowledgeable of the world.'

'Yes, but which world are we in now? I don't think this is Edinburgh.'

'Or Kansas.'

My giggle grew from the pit of my stomach and jumped out of my mouth.

'Are you quoting *The Wizard of Oz* to me?'

She stopped near the river's edge. 'It's one of my favourite movies. I like how all the bad people get their comeuppance.'

My ribs throbbed as I held on to them. 'My comeuppance is your tuppence. And tuppence will get you ten bob when fifty pee goes to the loo.'

'Skip, skip, skip to the loo, but only be careful and watch what you do because you don't want to step in any poo.'

We stared at each other, and then laughed in stereo.

Cassie held my arm as we peered into the water, fascinated by our reflections.

'There's something wrong with us.' I managed to get the words out so they made sense, but it was a struggle.

Cassie burped loud enough to scare the fish from the water.

'Wrong, gone, long, be bong pong.' She belched again before placing one hand on her mouth. 'Oops.'

I took a step back and sat in the grass before I fell into the river.

'There's something wrong, Cassie.'

She dropped down next to me with a thump. 'It's drugs.'

I held out my hand and saw my skin shimmering. 'What? How do you know?'

She grinned at me and tapped the side of her nose.

'Take it from one who knows.' Then she spewed out a huge laugh. 'Knows, geddit?'

I didn't, but couldn't help joining in with her crazy giggling. Our noise was so much we didn't hear the foot-steps approaching. Then somebody whispered behind us, so I bent my head back and tried to see who was there. A young girl, maybe eleven or twelve, with piercing blue eyes and shiny black hair peered down at me.

'Where did you two come from?'

Her voice was like a lullaby settling inside my head. It was impossible to stand, so I twisted around on the grass to face her. She had a friend with her, a girl about the same age with the same distinctive eyes, but with curly blonde hair. They wore long white dresses and appeared to float two inches above the grass.

'Are you fairies?' Cassie said.

'I'm Lily,' the dark-haired one said. 'And that's my sister Freda. We're people, just like you.'

Freda removed a large magnifying glass from somewhere and stuck it right up to my face.

'Are you sure these are people like us, Lily? They seem very different to me.'

'Different is good, Lily. It makes things more interesting.'

Freda pushed the magnifier on to my nose, so I felt the cold of the glass.

'These seem quite peculiar.'

Lily clapped her hands and my brain shook against my skull.

'Peculiar is even better. All the very best people are peculiar.'

Freda put the magnifier away, though I didn't see where.

'Like the man with two heads.'

'Exactly,' Lily said. 'And Fifty Foot Queenie, the Jean Genie, the Mayor of Simpleton, and Dagenham Dave.'

Cassie lay on her side and laughed. 'Dagenham's in London. I've been there.'

The girls sat next to us as Lily spoke. 'So have we, but we prefer it here.'

Freda touched my hair. 'I don't think you two should be here.'

I lifted my hand to look through my fingers, amazed at how all the rainbow colours turned into a group of unicorns and flew through pink clouds.

'Did you drug us?'

Lily caressed my cheek. 'No, silly. You're all confused because you shouldn't be in this place. Your bodies can't handle the atmosphere of this environment.' The sisters giggled together. 'You girls are wonderfully peculiar, but you're not peculiar enough. That's why you're all zonked out.'

Cassie twisted on to her side in slow motion. 'I think I'm going to throw up.'

Freda put one hand under Cassie's head and lifted her, while Lily did the same to me.

'Here, this will make you feel better.' They dropped a pill each into our mouths, and we swallowed automatically.

It trundled down my throat and rolled into my stomach as I gazed into the sky, watching the mystical rainbow animals wave at me with their hooves before disappearing. A spark of electricity sprang into my gut and I jolted upright.

I wiped the sweat from my forehead. 'You're right. I do feel better.'

Cassie jumped up. 'Me too.' She looked at the girls. 'What did you give us?'

Lily smiled at us. 'That's a secret. Perhaps you should tell us how you got inside a place you shouldn't get inside.'

My throat was drier than a sandbox and I was tempted to jump into the river.

'We came through an entrance at the Nelson Monument.'

Lily's smile disappeared as she glanced at her sister.

'Only special people can get through that.'

'Well, we're pretty special,' Cassie said.

'Not like us,' Freda said.

I rubbed at my throat. 'You're fairies, and we're...' I hesitated, not knowing how to finish that sentence. So Cassie did it for me.

'We're humans and we're looking for a Hellhound's earring. Do you know where it is?'

The girls took a step back from us. 'We don't know what

that is.' Lily said. 'But if it's an object of value, then the Collectors will have it.' She shivered when she said that name.

'And you want to keep away from them,' Freda said.

Cassie slapped the side of her as if she was knocking out the last of the magic this place had put there.

'Don't you worry about us, girls. My sister and I have dealt with a lot worse than a few people who collect things.' She smiled at them. 'Now, where are these Collectors?'

Lily shook her head. 'You don't understand. The Collectors only collect the most peculiar and wonderful things.'

'We know,' Cassie said. 'So we need the Hellhound's earring from them.'

Freda stepped forward. 'What my sister means is that once the Collectors see you two, they'll have to add you to their collection.'

I gulped. 'They collect living things?'

'The most peculiar and wonderful things, living or not,' Lily said.

Cassie slipped the blade from her jacket. 'I've dealt with people traffickers before. Human or supernatural, they all bleed the same way.' She ran her finger over the tip. 'Now tell us where we can find them.'

The girls pointed as one to the same spot. Cassie groaned and I shook my head.

'You should have learnt to swim, Sister.'

14   THE VALLEY OF THE DOLLS

'**B**loody typical!' Cassie's teeth grinding was loud enough, I'm sure it was heard beyond the mystical barrier and in the streets of Edinburgh.

'The Collectors live in the river?' I said to Lily.

The kid shrugged. 'Why not? It's as good a place as any.'

I didn't argue with that. 'How do they breathe?'

Freda stepped forward. 'Oh, that's easy. Halfway down, there's a ripple which takes you under the water and into the valley.'

'The valley?' I said.

'The valley of the dolls,' Lily said. 'They collect lots of different things, but they do love their dolls.'

Freda spun around, shook her hands in the air and danced a little jig.

'And they do have lovely dolls.'

Lily grimaced. 'Apart from the ones that bite.'

Freda stopped dancing. 'Yes, I hate those. Nasty little things, they are.'

Cassie puffed out her cheeks. 'So we swim to the

middle, and then we'll pass into this valley where we can breathe again?'

Lily shrugged. 'You might, and you might not. I mean, you shouldn't have been able to see the gateway and enter here, yet somehow you did.' She grinned. 'So yes, you might not drown.'

I sighed. 'Apart from the fact she can't swim.' I peered at Cassie. 'How do you get to sixteen without learning how to swim?'

Cassie threw her hands into the air. 'I moved around a lot, never staying in one place or school for too long. I guess I slipped between the cracks.'

I moved towards the river. 'I suppose I'll have to go on my own.'

She grabbed my arm. 'No way, Alice. Remember, we said nothing would separate us again. I'm not letting you go down there without me.'

I wriggled out of her grasp. 'Did you bring some breathing apparatus with you?'

Cassie glared at me. 'Of course not.'

'So, unless you want to drown, you're staying here.'

'But, Alice...'

'No buts, Cassie. We need the earring to get the Hellhound to take us to Hell to find our mother. Unless you have another way we haven't thought of?'

'We can help you,' the fairy girls said together.

I turned to them. 'How?'

Lily spoke. 'We'll guide your sister, Cassie, under the water until she reaches the ripple. All she needs to do is hold her breath.'

'How long for?' I said.

The sisters stared at each other and rolled their eyes before Lily answered.

'About two minutes.'

I spoke to Cassie. 'Can you do that?'

'Easy peasy,' she replied. 'How about you?'

'I used to go swimming every weekend. I'll be okay.'

Lily took Cassie's hand, then Freda the other.

'Are you ready?' Lily said.

Cassie grinned at me. 'As I'll ever be.'

Lily turned to me. 'Just follow us.'

They guided my sister into the river, and I went with them. The water was warmer than it looked, slipping over my legs and arms. I took a deep breath, then plunged under.

It was dark and I lost the three of them immediately. Before the panic kicked in, tiny lights like fireflies appeared a few feet away, and I swam towards them. When I got there, the illuminated dots were sparkling all along the bodies of Lily and Freda.

They guided Cassie down, and I stuck to their slipstream, never letting the illumination out of my sight. The heat in the water increased the further we went as if I was inside a giant Jacuzzi. The river didn't bubble around me, but a hum vibrating through it made my skin tingle.

We had been swimming for about a minute when it struck me that I'd never asked the girls if they'd wait for us while we spoke to the Collectors. I also considered what we'd do if they refused to give us the Hellhound's earring.

As those thoughts danced around my head, fish of many colours swam beside me: reds, yellows, greens, oranges, and blues gave me an aquatic guard of honour as we went deeper. I had perhaps thirty seconds of air left in my lungs as I saw a shimmering ripple ahead of us. Lily glanced at me and pointed at the anomaly with her free hand.

I allowed myself an underwater smile as something big knocked me sideways. My mouth sprang open, releasing the oxygen and letting in the river. Water rushed down my throat as the beast swam towards me with its vast teeth bared.

My arms splashed through the river. I managed to twist to the side, so the creature's head hit my elbow, but it didn't bite into me. I rolled through the water and away from the others as the creature came for me again. There was death in its eyes and my life in its mouth. My reflexes put one hand out as protection as the other grabbed at my throat.

I waited for an eternity for my life to flash before my eyes, my brain only staying awake because of the light show sparkling in front of me. With the whole of her body glowing like a shooting star, Lily fell on the beast, exploding a massive burst of energy that threw the monster far from us. As I watched it disappear, Freda grabbed my hand and dragged me into the abyss. I was just about out of air when she pulled me through the ripple.

My mouth sprang open as my head found air, and Freda dragged me from the water. She placed me on a patch of sand as Cassie ran to me. My chest was on fire with a vast expanding weight surging through me. She put her mouth to mine and sucked liquid out of me before blowing life back in. She did it three more times before I rolled on to my side and spat bits of the river all over dry land.

'Are you okay?' Lily stood over me, looking as if she was the adult in the room, or wherever it was we were.

Cassie helped me up as I spoke. 'I won't need a drink for a while.'

I shook the damp from my eyes and scanned our surroundings. It was very similar to the place we'd left, full of trees, bushes, grass and rolling hills. Only this was deep under a river. I rubbed the last bit of fluid from my lungs and wondered how bruised they'd be.

'Shall we take you to the Collectors?' Freda said.

'Lead on,' Cassie said.

Our feet squelched in unison, heading away from the river and towards the closest hill. Water dripped from me as we went.

'Are they nearby?'

Lily nodded. 'Not far, perhaps ten minutes away. Just keep an eye out for the dolls.'

Cassie glanced at me. 'Into the valley of the dolls, eh? Are these living dolls?'

Freda laughed. 'Of course. What would be the point of unliving dolls?'

Damp seeped from my socks and into my toes as I inched up to my sister.

'We stick to the plan when we meet these collectors.'

'We ask them kindly for the loan of the Hellhound's earring?'

'Yes, so I'll do all the talking.'

Cassie laughed. 'I hope you've brought all your charm with you, Alice.'

Before I could reply, Lily stopped in front of us. 'Oh, no.'

It didn't take long to see what had halted her. Heading straight towards us was a long line of walking dolls: they were all the same size, about twelve inches tall, with large heads spinning on their shoulders.

'What the...?' Cassie said.

Freda took her sister's hand. 'The Collectors only take the possessed ones. They have more fun with them.'

'Possessed by what?' I said.

Lily wiped a single tear from her eye. 'The dead. The dolls are possessed by the dead, with souls imprisoned inside their plastic bodies. A few of them are nice, but most are horrible.'

It was a dreadful sight, seeing them marching in a single line with those heads spinning constantly. 'Who imprisoned the souls?'

'Dark mages, magicians, wizards, witches; anyone who has the right artefact to create such terrible magic. Dolls have always been popular with those with twisted minds,' Freda said.

Cassie cracked her knuckles. 'I've seen those films, but we've nothing to worry about, yes?'

Lily stared at us. 'It depends on why they're here. Perhaps the Collectors are exercising their hoard, or....'

'Or what?' I said.

Her expression darkened. 'They know you're here, and why.'

'Okay,' Cassie said. 'What have we got to worry about from two dozen or so demonic killer dolls?'

As she spoke, the dolls stopped moving, with legs and heads stationary. They were about a hundred yards from us, close enough to see the darkness where their eyes should have been.

Lily whispered to me, 'Do you have weapons?'

Cassie and I had the blades in our hands before Lily finished the question. The doll at the front pulled away from the others and rushed at Cassie. She didn't appear too fussed until it lifted from the ground and jumped at her head. As my heartbeat increased, my sister thrust out her arm and plunged the knife into the doll's face.

The head split apart and let out an unholy scream. I put my hands over my ears as the doll crumbled to the floor, with bits of arms and legs tumbling into the grass.

Cassie wiped bits of the thing from the blade. 'See, that was easy.'

I wasn't too sure. The doll's remains twisted and moved on the ground as if it was trying to stitch itself back together. Then a low hum came from the others.

Freda placed one hand on her sister's arm. 'I think you've upset them.'

She must have been right as the hum increased until each doll opened its mouth to howl. And then they charged as a group.

'Form a circle,' Cassie said as she grabbed my arm. The fairy sisters joined us, but with no weapons. I worried about them. And then I remembered what they'd done under the water to the creature that attacked me.

Lily and Freda lifted their hands at the murderous toys speeding towards them. A rainbow shimmer of light sparkled in their palms before transforming into a burst of bright light. They pushed their arms out, and the light shot from them like bullets out of a machine gun, melting anything in its path.

I was relaxing somewhat, knowing the girls would keep us safe, when something landed on my chest. I crashed backwards and away from the others.

The ground was hard underneath me and a shock of electricity surged up my arm from my elbow. A weight pressed on my ribs and something snarled at me. I twisted my head to see burning yellow eyes and manic teeth. I brought my arm up just in time as the demon doll's long nails grasped for my face. They cut into my jacket as the fiend bit into my clothes.

I pushed up and tossed it away from me.

Then another hit me in the legs while one more landed on my shoulders. The one grabbing my legs pulled me to the ground while the other doll clawed at my neck. I rolled over the grass and shook the one trying to pull my eyes out. Then I reached down and punched the doll crawling up my body.

The head smashed into pieces, but it continued to pull itself along my trousers. I jumped up and kicked out my legs to get rid of it, but it was a persistent bugger, digging its sharp talons through the material and into my leg. I grabbed what was left of it and hauled it off me, dropped it to the ground, and then stamped it into pieces.

Those bits were still moving as I checked on the others. Lily and Freda were hugging each other while surrounded by melted dolls, but I couldn't see Cassie anywhere. There were broken bits of the possessed toys everywhere, but no sign of my sister.

Panic surged through me as I ran to the girls. 'Where's Cassie?'

They pointed beyond the mound of destruction, which continued to move amongst the grass. There was a shape lying there: Cassie.

15 SPELLBOUND

My heart thumped against my ribs as I ran to Cassie. Bits of broken dolls whined and twitched around me as I reached her. The low hum of demonic possession made my hair stand on end as I dropped to the ground, staring at my sister's closed eyes and unmoving body. My fingers shook as I reached for her, the ache in my heart heavy enough to drag me under the earth.

And then she snapped up and grinned at me.

'I needed a rest.' Her smile warmed every inch of me. 'Are you okay? And the girls?' She took my hand, and I helped her up.

'We're all fine.'

The destroyed dolls continued to hum around us. For one brief second, it reminded me of the university disco I was at before my journey into the supernatural began. Was that the last normal thing I did?

We went to Lily and Freda, glancing at the hot liquid bubbling near us as we reached the fairy girls. Cassie brushed the dust from her clothes.

'Will these Collectors send any more threats our way?'

Lily shrugged. 'I don't know, but the castle is just over the next hill.'

'The castle?' I said.

Freda nodded. 'They need somewhere big to keep their collection.'

We followed the girls as they led us over the hill, Cassie by my side and speaking in hushed tones.

'The Collectors obviously see us as enemies, so I'm not sure if your charm will work on them, Sister.'

She was right, but I had other things to consider, speaking as low as I could.

'If everyone here is a fairy, why are the girls helping us?'

We stared at Lily and Freda as they reached the top of the hill, Cassie looking as if she was about to answer my question when we saw the castle ahead. It was a magnificent sight, an ancient building so tall, the top of it reached into the clouds. There was no moat around it, only a giant statue guarding the entrance and a large meadow we strode through. Strange birds circled above us and the air smelt of honey.

It took two minutes to reach the feet of the great statue of a woman facing out from the castle with her vast arms held out as if ready to embrace the world. Lily and Freda knelt next to the stone, whispering something under their breath. They stayed like that for thirty seconds before standing again, and Freda spoke.

'This is Luluwa. All that we are comes from her.'

I ran my fingers over the stone. 'She's your queen?'

'Luluwa is the ancestor of us all,' Lily said.

'Will she protect us inside this castle?' Cassie said.

Lily shrugged and said nothing. Then the sisters led us inside. I glanced at Cassie, still wondering if this was some elaborate trap. We walked below the keep and into the courtyard. It was empty, apart from a few chickens wandering around and ignoring us. I assumed the girls had been here before as they took us into a long corridor. Tapestries covered the walls, with each of them depicting a battle or a victory, while large suits of armour provided a guard of honour as we progressed deeper into the castle.

The girls stopped at the end and turned to us.

'This is the main hall,' Freda said. 'We must wait for you out here.'

We left them and entered. Cassie's hand was close to the blade in her jacket as I scanned the room. More tapestries hung from the walls, joined this time by several large paintings of distinguished-looking men and women. A large fireplace was at the far end, but in between us and that was a table. Sitting at it was a woman.

'Come in, children. I won't bite you.'

Cassie stepped forward with the knife in her hand.

'Was it you who set those murderous dolls on us?'

The woman stepped from behind the table, with her long yellow and green dress swaying behind her. The way it moved was mesmerising, and the glittering jewels sewn into it like shimmering stars in the night sky magnetised me. Long red hair flowed down her back and over her shoulders. As she moved forward, I saw a loom behind her.

'Those dolls belong to the Collectors. I have no idea what they get up to.'

'You're not a Collector?' I said.

The air vibrated around her when she laughed. 'What need have I for such trivial items? I am Morgan le Fay, and the only thing which interests me is the mysteries of life.' She peered at me through shining green eyes. 'And you two are quite the mystery, aren't you?'

My fingers twitched as I spoke. 'Morgan le Fay? I know who you are.'

She laughed again, the sound making le Fay's hair quiver on her shoulders.

'I should hope everyone has heard of me, child.'

Cassie held the knife in her hand. 'I've never heard of you, lady, but if you give us what we want, I'll make sure to put your photo all over the internet.'

Morgan le Fay shook her head. 'You people and your obsession with modern things. You don't know what you've missed by abandoning the natural for the manufactured.' She stared at me. 'What is it you know about me, girl?'

The way she said it was more of a demand than a request, but I had to answer.

'If you genuinely are Morgan le Fay, you're connected to the myth of King Arthur and Camelot. Perhaps you're a goddess, a fay, a witch, or a sorceress.'

Cassie moved closer to the woman. 'Are you the Queen of the fairies?'

Le Fay shook her head. 'I'm many things to many people, child.' She wagged a jewelled finger at me. 'King Arthur and Camelot are not myths.' She glanced around the castle. 'Where do you think you are?'

I took a deep breath. 'This is Camelot?'

She nodded. 'What's left of it. I saved what I could when I brought it here.'

'This is all fascinating,' Cassie said, 'and I'm sure I've seen the film, but we're here for the Hellhound's earring.' She waved the knife at le Fay. 'Do you have it, or do we need to find these Collectors?'

Morgan le Fay narrowed her eyes, and it felt as if she contained the knowledge of the universe inside that sparkling green.

'A Hellhound's earring is a powerful artefact, child. Why do you want it?'

Cassie went to reply, but I put my hand on her arm to calm her nerves. There was no point annoying this woman, whoever she was, not when we needed her help.

'My sister and I have to enter the gates of Hell, for which we need a Hellhound and the earring. We've been told the dog is the transport, and the earring is the key to get in.'

Le Fay moved close to me and I smelt the aroma of lavender on her. The jewelled dress continued to glitter as she bent her head towards me, and I saw the rings in her ears.

'I have sisters as well, eight of them. But we were separated a long time ago, and it breaks my heart every day to think of where they are without me.'

I reached out for one of her earrings, but she moved back from me.

'Which one is it?'

Cassie pushed me to the side. 'I'll cut both of them from your head, lady.'

Morgan le Fay smiled at the threat. 'There's no need for that, child. I'll give you what you want if you give me something in return.'

She removed the ring from her right ear, a plain white circle you could have found in any cheap jewellery shop. Was that the one, or was this just a trick?

There was only one way to find out. 'What do you want for the earring?'

'That's the spirit, girl.' She continued to grin. 'But first, tell me why two sweet kids like you want to enter the gates of Hell.'

Perhaps she was playing with us for some strange

reason, but I answered anyway.

'The Queen of Hell stole our mother from us, and we're going to get her back, no matter what.'

'Come Hell or high-water,' Cassie said.

Sadness filled le Fay's face. 'Yes, having your family taken from you is the worst thing in the world.' She glanced around the castle. 'It's the worst thing in all the worlds.'

I saw her fighting back the tears and knew what she wanted.

'You want to be reunited with your sisters.'

Morgan le Fay nodded. 'More than anything in the world. I'd give anything for that, never mind one of Hell's trinkets.'

She threw the earring at Cassie, who caught it before it hit the floor. It also distracted Cassie enough to lower her other hand holding the knife, giving le Fay sufficient time to step in and knock it from my sister's fingers. Before I knew what had happened, she had her arm around Cassie's neck and was pulling her towards the table.

'What are you doing?' I shouted.

'Isn't it obvious?' she said. 'I'm taking your sister hostage, so you'll help me find mine.' She snatched the earring from Cassie's hand and threw it at me. I didn't fall for the same trick and let it hit the ground. 'You can have that since you're going to need it.'

'Why?'

'It isn't only a key into Hell. It's the original skeleton key constructed from the bones of the first archangel Lucy murdered after her fall from Heaven. It will open any door or gateway. The vampire who sent you here wants it for herself.'

I gripped my fingers into fists, trying not to think about more secrets and lies.

'Why does Vika want the Hellhound earring?'

Le Fay laughed at me as Cassie struggled in her grip. 'Think about it, child. That key will give her access to anything she wants, including this realm of the fairies. She doesn't care about you or your mother.'

'Why would Vika want to come here?' It was my turn to laugh. 'No offence, but no matter how pretty it is with the hills and the countryside, I think she prefers the temptations of the city.'

'Your vampire doesn't want to come here for the views, child. She wants those children who brought you here, them and all the others like them.'

'Why?' It didn't make sense to me. What would Vika get here she couldn't find in the human world? And then it hit me. 'Blood. She wants fairy blood.'

Le Fay increased her grip on Cassie and I watched my sister's cheeks bulge.

'Fairy blood is much richer than human blood, with a far sweeter taste. It also gives the vampire more strength than any other blood from the human or supernatural world. That's why she wants the key to here. And she tricked you into coming for it.'

It sounded plausible, but I still didn't trust her, especially since she was choking the life from my sister.

'Let Cassie go and I promise to help you find your sisters.'

She pondered my words for so long, I thought I'd have to rush her before Cassie died. Then she let go and pushed her towards me. I grabbed on to Cassie and waited for an attack, but it never came.

Cassie rubbed at her throat and spat out her words. 'I'm going to kill you for that.'

Morgan le Fay dismissed the threat with a wave of her

hand. 'Sometime in the future, I'll call on you for your promise, Alice Arcane, but for now, you should leave this realm while you still can.'

'How do you know my name?'

'Your fame precedes you, child.' She pointed behind her. 'But can you hear that?'

I hadn't until she waved her finger at it, but I could now, even though Cassie gritting her teeth put my nerves on edge. It was an echoing howl getting closer.

'What is it?'

Le Fay laughed. 'If I didn't need you in the future, I'd leave you to their fury, but I can't have that. You destroyed their precious dolls, and now the Collectors want their revenge.'

'Let then come.' Cassie spat the words out. 'I'll kill them, and then you.'

I grabbed the earring from the floor. 'Come on. We got what we came for. There's no point hanging around.' The fire burning in her eyes warmed my cheeks. 'It's not worth the risk, Cassie. Think of our mother.'

That reminder must have convinced her as she turned for the way we'd come in, but not without one last glare at Morgan le Fay. I had one final look myself, and she smiled at me.

'We'll meet again, Alice, and you'll need all your strength then to return my sisters to me.'

I slipped the earring into my pocket and left without a reply. The howling was louder and closer now. I ran to the exit, catching up with Cassie and finding Lily and Freda waiting for us in the corridor.

Lily was biting her fingernails. 'This isn't good.'

The three of them ran ahead of me as a chill breath settled on the back of my neck.

16 EVE OF DESTRUCTION

I stumbled outside and fell, my palms hitting the hard grass as I rolled over to stare at what followed me. But there was nothing there.

Cassie helped me up. 'Are you okay, Alice?'

I stared beyond her, trying to see whatever had chased us, but even the howling had disappeared. Did I dream that touch on the back of my neck?

'Where are the girls?'

She let go of me and nodded behind us. 'There they are.'

The sisters stood at the feet of the statue, their faces frozen in horror. Lily turned to me.

'Luluwa is upset with you.'

'It's okay, kid,' Cassie said. 'We're not afraid of a piece of rock.'

And then the rock moved. It was one leg at first, creaking as it lifted from the ground and stamped a foot towards us. Great mounds of dirt jumped in the air from the vibration and settled over my face. I sneezed as the statue moved its other leg and ripped parts of the ground away.

I grabbed Cassie and stepped back. 'I think it's time for us to go.'

But she was frozen in my grip as the concrete Luluwa bent its head towards us and spoke from stone lips.

'You have offended my children, outlanders, and now you must pay the price.'

Luluwa swiped her grey fingers at my face before I could move, my head only staying on my shoulders because Cassie was fast enough to pull me away. We staggered back as the statue creaked and stumbled. If it had ever walked before, I assumed it must have been a long time ago since it faltered on its concrete legs.

'Run!' Lily shouted as she and Freda sprinted ahead of us. We did as she said, with Cassie pulling me with her. I didn't look back, but heard the stone moving along the earth.

'We can't outrun it,' I said as we fled.

Cassie gripped my hand. 'We've got no choice, Alice.'

The ground vibrated under us like an earthquake, with dust and dirt jumping up as the statue found its feet. I let go of Cassie, stopped and turned. We'd got two hundred yards or so from Luluwa, but she, it, would catch us soon enough.

'If we run, it'll catch us, and then we're dead.' It had gained fifty yards on us in a few seconds.

'Crap,' Cassie said. 'So what do we do?'

Another fifty yards went by in a heartbeat. 'We have to topple it.'

The dirt rumbled below us. 'And how do we do that?'

'We improvise.' The words slipped from my lips as the living statue swung a giant fist at me. It was quick, but still not fast enough in its concrete form to catch me as I slipped to the side and rolled behind it. It swung again, this time at Cassie, but she was as agile as me.

'We haven't got anything to drag it down,' she shouted as it turned to face us. And that's when the idea hit me.

'We need to get it over the hill.' I sprinted from its grasp and headed for the point where Lily and Freda watched us.

Cassie was at my side as I scrambled up. 'Then what do we do?'

The statue groaned behind us as it stomped through the earth.

'Don't worry, Sis, you'll see.'

Great grey fingers swiped at my legs as I skipped away from Luluwa, running for the fairy sisters and glancing at Cassie at my side. We dodged the still twitching remains of the broken dolls as the statue crushed them under its feet.

And then I saw what we needed as the others sprinted to the side. I stopped and turned, making sure the statue still pursued us. It picked bits of plastic from its toes, yet somehow managed to glare at me from concrete eyes. It didn't move, so I decided to motivate it.

'Are you part of the collection?'

'I am beyond your comprehension, child.' Its voice sounded like broken glass in a blender.

'You're not Luluwa, are you? You're just an automaton the Collectors added to their toys. Somewhere in that castle, they're pushing buttons to get you to move, and there isn't an original thought in your stone head.'

It picked up a bunch of twitching dolls' heads and crushed them between its fingers. The bits dropped to the ground, but it still didn't move towards me. I assumed behind its eyes were cameras broadcasting to its controllers back in that castle.

'The human world will be no more soon, girl. You and your sister could stay here with us. You'd be the highlight of our collection.'

'What do you mean the world will be no more?'

'Wheels have been in motion for longer than you've been alive, Alice Arcane. Nobody can stop the destruction, not even the Children of the Nephilim. This is why you should stay here in our collection. Even when you're dead, we can reanimate your corpses to take pride of place in our exhibition. There will be no more suffering for you, no more loneliness, only peace.'

I struggled to control my breathing. 'How do you know who I am?'

'The Queen of Camelot knows all and tells us what we need.'

'What is Morgan le Fay to you?'

Something crackled in its throat that I would have sworn was an attempt at laughter.

'That woman? She allows us residence in the castle for services rendered.'

'What services?'

'Why should we tell you anything, girl?'

I shrugged. 'Consider it my last request before you kill me.'

The statue took one giant step towards me and its stone foot landed heavily amongst the broken dolls.

'We service punishment on those who have wronged her. In return, we get to store our collection in the eternal halls of Camelot.'

'Well, Morgan is our friend now, and I don't think she'd be happy with you hurting my sister or me.'

'It's too late for that, child. You destroyed our precious dolls and will be punished for that.'

It lunged at me with both arms outstretched. It was close, but not enough to grab me as I dived to the side, and the statue landed in the middle of the dolls Lily and Freda had melted earlier. I rolled to the side and watched it struggle to get up.

Cassie helped me up again. 'That won't hold it for long.'

'It will be enough for us to get out of here.'

I glanced at its giant stone body grappling in the molten mess as I ran with Cassie and caught up to Lily and Freda by the side of the river.

'You need to take another deep breath,' Lily said.

I peered at my reflection in the water. 'It's the same as before? We dive in, and then swim down and we'll come out on the other side?' The girls nodded. 'What about the creature that attacked me last time?'

Lily held up her hands. 'I think we scared it away. It won't try anything like that again.'

Behind us, the statue roared. It was the spring we needed, with the girls guiding Cassie into the water first. I didn't look back as I followed them. It was dark for only a second, with shimmering, glowing lights around the others leading me down into the river. Once again, it felt strange to think I was swimming down, knowing I'd be coming up at the other end.

It was quicker this time to reach the ripple. Watching Lily take Cassie through while Freda waited for me, I took her hand and let her pull me up, our heads puncturing the water together. I gasped for air as it rushed into me before crawling on to land and lying next to my sister. Lily and Freda hugged while Cassie grinned at me.

'I hope you didn't lose the key, Alice.'

I spat water to the side and reached into my pocket, finding the earring and removing it. A shiver trickled down my damp spine as I remembered it was bone.

'We got what we came for, so let's not waste any more time here.'

Cassie laughed as she lay next to me. 'Yeah, that rumble in your guts isn't a good sign.'

I put a hand on my stomach. 'That wasn't me.'

But the sound increased, turning into a roar as the surface of the river trembled, the water rippling like jelly in a microwave. Then it split asunder, and something leapt out of it, landing between us as we were drenched. I rubbed the water from my face and stared at something from a movie: a humanoid figure covered in scales, with gills. It was a fishman.

'Give me the key, child.'

Heat burnt behind my eyes as I stood, sick of being called a child.

'Did the Collectors send you?'

He laughed through his gills. 'I hate them. What they have isn't a collection, but a prison, and I'm one of their many prisoners. I owe you thanks for distracting them enough for me to slip away, but I need that key to complete my escape from here.'

Cassie stood next to me. 'What do you mean about a prison?'

He turned to her. 'They take living things and imprison them. What more do you need to know?'

I gripped the key. 'How many prisoners are there?'

'Including me, more than a hundred.' His scales trembled as he spoke. 'Now give me that key.'

I glanced at Cassie, a split second hesitation which was our undoing. The fishman grabbed us both, scaly fingers around my neck before I could respond.

'Let them go,' Lily shouted.

He shook his head as he squeezed my throat. 'I think not, fairy. But I'll kill them both if you or the other one try any of your tricks.'

Then he switched his attention to the bone earring still between my fingers. Since he held on to Cassie and me, he couldn't grab the key, until he tossed her away and reached over for it.

His fingers were above mine when something else burst out of the river. Two long metallic strands shot towards the fishman, wrapping themselves around his legs and snaking up his body, reaching his neck. They strangled the protest in his throat as they hauled him back into the water after he'd dropped me.

He disappeared with a whoosh as I rubbed at my neck. Cassie was at my side as the river bubbled and the fishman vanished into it.

'I'm beginning to dislike this place,' she said.

'It's normally lovely here,' Lily said, 'but perhaps you two should leave as soon as possible.'

I agreed. 'I can't remember where it was we came in. How do we get out?'

She pointed at the bone ring in my hand. 'You have more ways now.'

'Which way do we go?' Cassie said.

Lily took my hand. 'Our house will do.' Freda grabbed Cassie, and they led us away from the river and into the trees. Squirrels and rabbits scattered before us as we entered the woods. The trail was direct to a cottage fifty yards in front of us.

My legs throbbed as we reached it, stumbling inside after Freda opened the door. She pointed to another door at the back.

'Place the key against that, then open it, and you'll return to Edinburgh.'

Cassie took the key from me and went to the door as I held the hands of the sisters who'd helped us.

'What will happen to you once we're gone?'
'Don't worry about us,' Lily said. 'We'll be fine.'
I hugged both girls as we said our farewells.
'Cassie and I will be back, I promise you.'
I pressed the key against the door.
And then we stepped through.

17 FAITH

We reappeared in the grounds of Vika's mansion, surrounded by the impressive topiary. A large bush cut into the shape of a dragon loomed over me as I stepped into the garden. I bent over and clutched at my chest.

Cassie ran to me. 'Are you okay, Alice?'

I lifted my face to her. 'How many have we left behind now?'

'You're talking about what the fishman told us is in the Collectors' prison?'

I twisted my head to get some of the pain out of it, but it didn't work.

'It seems everywhere we go, people are oppressed or suffering, and we can't do anything about it.' I forced down the roaring in my chest. 'What's the point of being the so-called Children of the Nephilim if we can't use the powers we're supposed to have to help others?'

She took my hand. 'I'm not sure what we're supposed to be, Alice, or if everyone has lied to us about our lineage. Something was different in Limbo, but perhaps that was more to do with the place than us.' She gripped my fingers. 'All I know now is the connection we have and that we need to find our mother. Once we've done that, we can consider what to do about those left behind on our journey.'

I let go of her and removed the bone earring from my pocket.

'And what about this? What if everything we've done has all been about getting this from Morgan le Fay?'

'What do you mean?'

'Maybe somebody planned this whole thing just to get us into the fairy realm because we're the only people capable of getting through the doorway. And all to get this key. It not only gets its owner into Hell, but through any door. The holder of this can go anywhere anytime they want.'

'That doesn't make sense, Alice. Nobody manipulated me into leaving Newcastle to go to Middlesbrough, where we found each other.'

'You don't think it's possible you were set up with that werewolf in Newcastle, so you'd follow it, and it led you to me?'

She shook her head. 'No, I don't. But even if that was true, how would this mystery conspiracy get us to go to Lindisfarne, and then the Nexus, which led us to Kai in Whitby?'

I threw the earring to the ground. 'I don't know. It's the supernatural, so isn't anything possible? Maybe there's some magical mastermind somewhere sitting in front of a crystal ball and manipulating us like chess pieces, so we end up exactly where they want us.'

She bent down to retrieve the key. 'I think you're over-thinking this, Alice, brought on by stress and the things we've seen and done. To get me from Newcastle to you, and then both of us through every place we've been to would take an enormous amount of power and control.'

She was right, which meant it could only be one person.

'Lucy could do it. God's former favourite, the First of the Fallen, could have manipulated us into all of this.'

'If that's so, why was she desperate to abduct us in the hospital when we went back in time?'

I scowled at the green dragon I thought was judging me. 'She's the Devil. How can we know how her mind works? Maybe that wasn't even the archangel Michael at the hospital, and all that guff about the Children of the Nephilim was nothing but lies.'

Tiredness and frustration were eating me up. I needed sleep, but if I closed my eyes, I didn't know what I'd awaken to. Cassie must have recognised it all in my face.

'Okay, let's say that's true. Why would she or anyone else have done this?'

I pointed at the key. 'I told you, she wants that.' A lightbulb went off in my head. 'Think about it, Cassie. What's the thing the Devil hates the most?'

She shrugged. 'People believing she's male?'

'No. God threw Lucy out of Heaven. Everything that followed, all the terrible things she's done and the demons, stems from that point. With that key, she has a way back there.' It all made sense to me now. 'God has left Heaven. That's what the archangels told us. With that key, Lucy can return there to rule over it.'

Cassie stared at the earring. 'If that's true, it means both Kai and Vika are involved and have lied to us.'

Even though I'd doubted Kai several times since we'd met, I didn't believe the Warwitch had lied to us.

'No, I think Kai has probably been manipulated just like we have.'

Cassie held the bone key up to the moonlight. 'So what do we do now?'

I took it from her. 'We continue as if nothing has happened. We still need to rescue our mother, and we need the Hellhound for that. So let's go and get him.'

We marched into the mansion, finding it empty of party-goers, but the mess everywhere was evidence of what had happened in the building. It smelt of booze and drugs as we headed back downstairs. The silence was eerie and prickled the hairs on my arms. Cassie went through the doors first, where we found Vika and Kai playing cards.

The vampire greeted us with a warm smile as the Hellhound sat at her feet.

'Well, that was quick. How was the land of the fairies?'

'Interesting,' I said. 'So how do we get to Hell?'

Vika knelt, tickled Scooby's chin and whispered something into his ear. Then they both stood.

'Drop the earring, and it will do the rest.'

Cassie and I looked at each other, knowing this was the key moment in more ways than one. Was this where Vika took the earring to give it to Lucy? Was the Devil already with us in the room?

My hesitation was brief, and I let go of the key. I waited for it to drop to the floor or disappear, but it did neither, floating through the air and settling on the Hellhound's ear.

'Cool,' I said. 'What now?'

Vika smiled at me. 'All you need is a leap of faith. Take hold of Scooby's fur, and he'll lead you into Hell. Kai and I will conclude our dealings here.' She patted the hound one last time. 'Best of luck, girls, and I hope you get what you want.'

I was at Scooby's side with my hand on his back; Cassie did the same on the other flank. The dog walked towards the far end of the room, and we went with him, the green fur bristling between my fingers. I expected the wall to move and a door to appear, but it didn't; it was the three of us who vanished.

Then everything was on fire around me.

WE REAPPEARED into a place of heat and frost, on a bridge between extremes. On one side were great snow clusters rising into a dark sky as giant ice-covered trees towered over us. On the other were large columns of flames, the heat scorching the air as we landed. Howls of humanity burst forth from both sides.

Scooby stood still and waited for us to move. I let go of his hide and inched towards the cold, my skin shrivelling in the temperature. A fine fog drifted over the edge of the bridge, allowing me a clear sight of below: a frozen sea enclosed most of the ground, while along its never-ending shore were corpses as far as the eye could see. A humongous shadow slithered near them from the icy bushes.

Cassie's hand was in mine. 'I hope Mother isn't down there.'

The shadow reared its gigantic skull, the snake baring long, ice-sharpened teeth, then dipping its head to devour the dead. I pulled away from Cassie, walking past Scooby and to the other side of the bridge. The heat melted the cold clinging to my flesh and bones as fire rained from the sky, falling into a burning lake. Next to it, giant horned creatures dangled children into the flames. The screams burnt my ears, and I fell into the Hellhound and away from my sister.

'Where do we start?'

Despair possessed me. A cloud of buzzing insects flew

at us, only twisting back when Scooby lifted his great head and growled at them.

Cassie placed a hand on Scooby's neck.

'We ignore what's below and keep walking until something prompts us to go in one direction or another.'

It was as good an idea as any. We strode forward, Scooby's low snarl a comfort to me as we moved over the bridge. An arctic wind blew in from one side, a sirocco heat from the other. I tried to shut my ears to the howling cries of the tortured and the shrieking of the tormentors, but it was impossible. I spoke to Cassie as the only way of reducing that noise.

'Do you think those people we saw on the boat in Limbo ended up here?'

'I hope not, but if this is Hell, then I guess Lucy is gathering souls for more than just her amusement.'

As she finished, so did the bridge, and we came to a complete halt, a sheer drop into an abyss. I hung on to Scooby's neck as I peered over the edge, the darkness shouting out to me, but I couldn't see into the bottom.

Cassie placed her hand on my shoulder.

'Can you hear the voices?'

I leant into Scooby's green hide, desperate to find comfort.

'They're calling my name.'

'Mine too.'

It was a familiar sound. 'Just like in Purgatory.'

Cassie looked everywhere around us. 'Do you think this is the same place, but a different part of it?'

I peered deep into Scooby's eyes. 'No, I trust our new friend to have brought us to the right place.'

'So what do we do next?'

My lungs ached as I sucked in the air, a toxic combination of death and despair. Vika's words came back to me.

'We need to take a leap of faith.' I stroked Scooby's head as I peered at Cassie.

'You want us to jump down there?' Her eyes were wide in amazement.

'It's that, or we turn around.' The temptation to do that nearly overwhelmed me.

Cassie looked at Scooby. 'What do you think, puppy; should we take a leap of faith off this bridge?'

Scooby pushed his large legs up and down in a rhythmic motion, his gigantic nose flaring and snorting a disgusting yellow gas into the abyss. Then he knelt and offered us his shaggy green back.

'I guess that's a yes.'

I climbed on to him. Cassie followed, grabbing my hips as we sucked air into our lungs. The noise hammering in my heart was matched by the banging in my skull. The Hellhound rose, energy vibrating through his powerful legs and spreading through me.

Cassie leant into the back of my neck. 'We're the Children of the Nephilim, and this darkness can't harm us.'

I had no time to reply before Scooby took that leap of faith.

It was a head-first dive, the wind blowing through my hair, those whispers growing louder the further we fell. I ignored them as light burst through the gloom, images appearing on either side of us: bodies were blown violently back and forth, their faces contorted and sliced by elements we couldn't see. Then they were swept above, screaming into the abyss as we kept on falling.

Next, freezing rain washed over me, the cold searing my skin as thousands of tiny worms flew through the storm. I wanted to shout as they headed for us, but we were of no interest to them, their slimy mouths settling on the doomed humans hovering in that space.

The harshness of the weather disappeared as we descended further. More people appeared on either side, groups of them eating each other in a never-ending circle of greed and gluttony. I recognised some from homes I'd lived in, adults with contorted, anguished faces. They ate flesh and bones in a terrible frenzy, only for them to regrow and go through the same process again.

We seemed to hover in the air, fixed in that spot to watch the horrors unfold in front of us. Then those terrible humans stopped feasting on each other.

And they turned to us.

18 HIGHWAY TO HELL

Cassie gripped on to me as we kept falling before the fiends attacked. She screamed into my ears, but the roar of our descent meant I couldn't hear anything. Around us, people tore at each other's faces, their skin burning red and their eyes bulging from their skulls. I glanced at Cassie, worried by the fire I witnessed inside her pupils, while a tingling sensation ran through my arms. Her nails bit into my hips like knives. I leant forward, pushing harder into Scooby's fur and forcing him into greater speed, turning my face away from the horrors around us.

The violence vanished as quickly as it had appeared, disappearing into the dark as Cassie relaxed her hold on me. A bright light surged towards us as we dropped through a crowd of flaming forms. The flames were in human shape, with melting, twisting faces peering deep into me. The heat was so intense, it dried the rain from me as burning skulls shrieked in agony.

And on we went, my mind wanting it to stop, my lungs gasping for oxygen. Centaurs and harpies flew around us, tearing apart whatever human bodies they grabbed in that eternal void. Heads were pulled from screaming adults and children, then tossed into the air like footballs. Limbs floated nearby as we fell, bouncing off Scooby's frame and heading into the direction we'd come from, rushing upwards to defy the laws of gravity.

I reached into my mind to find comfort in my science knowledge, but nothing could soothe the utter horror around us.

A giant winged beast with three heads, six hands and six feet containing nails as long as medieval swords hovered, in front of me. On the end of each talon was a speared human, their faces contorted into agony. The creature swallowed one person at a time, with their place taken by another body appearing out of nothing on its claws.

As my mind screamed for release, we hit the ground, Scooby bracing his legs so we didn't crumble into a heap. The darkness was gone and pure snow surrounded us on the mountains. As we jumped off the Hellhound, my feet landed on a frozen lake; cold gripped me as I shivered next to Cassie. I stroked Scooby's fur to spark some warmth into my hands and remove what I'd witnessed from my mind.

A frosty terrain stretched out ahead. 'This could take forever.'

'We might not last that long.' Cassie pointed forward, beyond the pure whiteness and into a massive dark cloud approaching. It appeared to move from side to side as it slid along the arctic path in our direction. Bits of it split apart into stretched sinewy tendrils scuttling towards us: slithers of shaggy darkness which weren't coils of smoke, but hairy legs supporting the bodies of dozens of giant spiders. Even from this distance, I saw their vast mouths possessed of drool-dripping fangs.

I turned to search for an escape route, only to find a wall

of sheer ice. The chill running through my body had nothing to do with the sub-zero conditions. Scooby sneezed and the ground shuddered. Maybe the Hellhound could eat what was coming for us. Willowing wafts of sulphur moved above the heads of the giant spiders as they kept on charging forward, the stink in the air making my lungs shiver and shrivel until it was hard to breathe.

I grabbed Cassie's hand. 'How do we fight our way out of this?'

If ever we needed to be the Children of the Nephilim, it was now. I searched deep inside me for the strength I'd had in Limbo, but it wasn't there.

The Devil had lied to us after all.

The swarm of spiders were nearly upon us, only a few feet away, their burning yellow eyes stinging my skull. My fingers tugged into Scooby's thick fuzz of fur as he sneezed again. As giant arachnid jaws lunged at me, he sneezed for the third time, and everything went white. A blinding flash forced me to push my hands over my face and cover my head. My legs froze as I expected the attack to land on me, but all that happened was a large gust of wind blew me back from the protection I sought from the Hellhound.

An aroma of sweet petals hit me as I removed my fingers from my head, staring not at a surge of murderous spiders, but a wall of vivid purple flowers sitting on spiky stalks: thistles. If we were still in Hell, it was the most beautiful part of it. Spectacular mountains surrounded us as we stood mesmerised in fields of blossoms. The ice and the spiders had vanished, or, I guessed, we'd been transported some-where else; but how?

'I think the big dog sneezed us to another location,' Cassie said.

Thick mist descended from the mountains, the chatter

of strange birds disappearing into the floating grey. I patted the Hellhound on the head.

'Well done, Scooby.' I didn't know where we were, but it had to be better than that other place.

'What now, Sister?'

Before I could answer, three figures stepped from the mist. Scooby shivered and bent his massive frame before them. They were women, identical in shape and face, with long, flowing blonde hair and green eyes like magnets to the lead in my legs. I wasn't sure if they moved closer to us or we strode towards them. One of them had a book in her hand, another clutched a knife, while the one in the middle held her arms out to me as she spoke.

'Welcome to this hidden land, Children of the Arcane.'

She stepped forward and placed her fingers on my forehead. I couldn't resist, my body under her control. She touched there for only ten seconds, but when she moved away, there was strength back inside my veins. I felt my head and the scar had disappeared.

'What did you do?' I said.

Light glistened around her. 'I am Brigid the Healer. These are my sisters, Brigid the Poet and Brigid the Smith.' Brigid the Poet handed me her book, while Brigid the Smith gave Cassie her knife. 'These will help you on your journey beyond this place.'

Cassie ran her fingers over the handle of the blade. 'It's always nice to get a new weapon.'

I slipped the small book into my pocket. 'Is this Hell?'

The sisters glanced at each other as if I'd said the funniest thing in the world.

'This is the Doon and what you seek is near here. Follow the path through the purple haze to complete your quest.'

As she spoke, the mist evaporated to reveal a trail that wasn't there earlier. Before Cassie or I could reply, the identical triplets slipped into the vapour and vanished.

'Well, this is much better than facing down a horde of carnivorous giant spiders, but I'm not sure if we should trust them.' Cassie examined the knife in great detail. 'But this feels special. Do you think we should follow this route?' She pointed the blade at the gap between the thistles.

A crescendo of bells rang through the heavens as I answered her question by walking towards the path.

'It's better than anything else.'

Cassie and Scooby joined me, the mist disappearing behind as we strode through the field of purple. An aroma of exotic fruit sprang from the flowers.

As we walked, I flipped through the book Brigid the Poet had given me. I furrowed my eyebrows as I stared at all the blank pages, wondering what its purpose was. Cassie talked to Scooby as we followed the sound of the bells. After five minutes, we exited the florae to find a classic British pub standing in front of us.

'The Fire and Brimstone,' Cassie said. 'That's not too subtle.'

Its brickwork was all scorched red, the top of it reaching so far into the sky, I couldn't see the end. There were tables and chairs outside, occupied by people arguing with each other. As we got closer, I recognised some faces: infamous killers from human history. Stalin shouted at Hitler, while Ted Bundy harassed a small bloke I didn't recognise. Cassie moved forward with her new weapon gripped in her hand. The men stopped shouting at each other and focused on us.

I stared at Stalin and forced him to turn away; whether it was Scooby or I who terrified him, it didn't matter.

'I guess we go inside.'

The doors were of the swinging type transported from the Wild West. I pushed them apart and marched in. It wasn't a surprise to see Lucy sitting at a table, her face like an exploding star. Our presence didn't faze her and she continued to deal cards to her four female companions.

'You girls took a fine time getting here; did you get lost?'

I gripped Cassie's arm as she went to lunge at the Queen of Lies.

'Not yet,' I said to her.

'Would you like to meet my friends?' Lucy finished dealing and held out her arms.

'Let's keep her talking,' I whispered to Cassie. We had no plan to deal with Lucy, nor were we sure our so-called Arcane abilities could defeat her. They hadn't appeared in Purgatory when I'd searched inside myself for them, or when we were facing down the killer spiders not so long ago.

Cassie strode ahead. 'I've always wanted to be a pirate.'

Lucy's grin was wide enough to stretch across the horizon.

'You have good taste, Cassandra Arcane, and these are two of the finest pirates of any era. This is Anne Bonny and Mary Read.' Bonny's flame-red hair sparkled on her shoulders, her face a construction of intense focus. Read was smaller, with shorter, darker hair and a mischievous leer in her eyes.

I stared beyond them, finally recognising the woman on Lucy's left, whose heavy eyelids couldn't detract from her Hollywood beauty. Maybe the pirates were here because of their notorious past, but she shouldn't be.

'What's Hedy Lamarr doing with you?' I asked.

'Who?' Cassie said.

'She's a movie legend and the inventor of wireless

communication; a woman whose scientific achievements were hidden for years.' I knew nothing of her film career, but as a scientist she was legendary.

Lucy put her arm around Hedy's shoulder. 'Who else would I use to fix my Wi-Fi problems? You wouldn't believe how bad the reception is here.'

'Who's your other stooge?' Cassie pointed her knife at the young woman in the figure-hugging art-deco dress smoking a cigar. She stood and aimed two pistols at my sister. Lucy was quick to make her lower the guns.

'Now, now, girls. As much as I like you, Cassandra Arcane, I don't think you'd come out on the right side of a fight with Bonnie Parker.' She turned her gaze to me. 'We're all women who've been wronged by male authority in this universe. I believe we can work together to correct the passage of history, don't you?'

I wouldn't play another one of her games. 'Where's our mother?' My fingers trembled, a surge of unexpected energy making me feel like a human battery.

There was an intriguing flicker behind Lucy's eyes.

'Mary Arcane was here, but she isn't anymore.'

Cassie inched forward. 'Then, you die now.' The blade from Brigid the Smith glowed in her grasp. Lucy flinched from it before holding up her hand.

'We can fight, but it won't achieve anything, and I need both of you alive, so I'll offer you a deal instead.'

Could Cassie and I defeat the Morningstar, and then force her to show us where our mother was? It seemed unlikely.

'What deal do you mean?'

The four women sat at the table while Lucy smiled at me. 'If you, Alice Arcane, beat me at one hand of poker, I'll tell you where your mother is.'

I didn't hesitate to reply. 'What happens if you win?'

'You stay with me, my slave for as long as you live, while your sister does the same with Michael. It's the only way of curtailing his apocalyptic plans and keeping the balance of power.'

Never deal with the Devil. Isn't that what all the myths and legends say? But this wasn't a myth or legend; this was real.

Cassie sidled up to me.

'We can't listen to her lies.'

I pressed my face close to hers. 'Do you believe we're strong enough to defeat her, and then make her reveal where our mother is? I feel different, but I'm not sure if even the two of us could overthrow the Devil in her domain.'

'Scooby could help.'

I glanced at the big, shaggy dog. 'No, I think he was used to lead us here, but I'd guess his loyalty rests with only one person.'

Cassie frowned. 'Can you beat her at poker?'

'I've never played cards in my life,' I said as I strode towards the Queen of Lies.

'I've never played poker before, so you'll have to deal a few practice hands to teach me the rules.'

Lucy continued to smile. 'Of course, Alice. I wouldn't want this to be an unfair contest.'

I sat at the table, watching Scooby's wide watery eyes peering at me. Nobody spoke as we played, apart from indicating what they were doing with their cards and Lucy explaining the rules. Every time it seemed as if I didn't understand what she meant, I could see Cassie cringing. Perhaps it was because I spent more time staring at the bone earring Scooby wore than the cards in my hand, thinking of all those I'd left to suffer to get to this point.

They dealt six rounds, with the Queen of Lies winning every time. After each hand, the cards were turned over and returned to the bottom of the pack unshuffled. Her eyes sparkled as she peered at me.

'Just the two of us at the table now, Alice.'

Bonnie Parker stood while the pirates and Hedy left their places. I stared at the Devil across the table as she dealt.

'What do you think will happen to Cassie and me as we get older?'

Lucy glanced at her cards as she spoke, her eyes flicking between them and me.

'Human potential and archangel power should make you creatures of unbridled ferocity. That's what the prophecy says.'

I laughed at prophecies coming true, but that wasn't the most important thing she'd said.

'You're saying we have archangel blood in our veins, not just your normal angel; that our grandfather was one of your siblings?' I hadn't looked at my cards yet.

Lucy let out a long sigh. 'Unfortunately, that is the case.'

'Who was it?'

'I'm not at liberty to say.'

I picked up the cards. 'I'll take one.' I discarded a king face down.

Lucy pushed it to the side. 'I'll keep what I have.'

She placed her cards on the table while the others watched. Cassie was a short distance away, holding Scooby. Would he sneeze her out of here if I lost? I smiled at the Hellhound.

'If you win, will you put me in a cage and torment me for the rest of eternity?'

The Morningstar fluttered her eyelashes at me. 'Don't be silly. I'll teach you how to refine your talents, and then we'll make sure Michael does nothing stupid to the planet.'

'I thought you said if I lost this game, Cassie would be his slave? Won't he do the same and use her as a weapon of mass destruction?'

Lucy tapped her fingers together. 'I'm afraid only one of you girls gets to live today.' She clapped her hands, and Bonny and Read pulled swords from thin air and held them at either side of Cassie's throat. All Scooby could do was lie on the floor and moan.

I focused all my attention on my opponent. 'You lied to me.'

She shrugged. 'Did you expect anything different? In the human realm, I could have taken you both by force, but in here, in my domain, certain rules have to be followed. I can't control a soul, even one as unusual as yours, without a bargain being struck.' Her smile revealed teeth whiter than a blank piece of paper. 'And here we are now.'

'Why would you kill Cassie?'

Lucy let out a long sigh. 'It's not by choice, believe me, but the potential of the two of you is off the chart; together, I think you could defeat even me. Trying to control both of you is too dangerous, and I can't take the risk of letting one of you fall into Michael's hands.' She picked at her cards, flipping the edges between her fingers and snapping the plastic on to the table.

'So, that claim of moderating the balance of power with me here with you and Cassie with Michael was another deception?'

'What can I say? I'm a product of my impulses.'

She turned over her cards all at once, a single king surrounded by four aces.

'Does someone as deceitful as you stick to your word once a bargain is set?'

Lucy pursed her lips and looked offended. 'No human would ever sell their soul to me if they thought I'd renege on the deal. They know I'll try to trick them somehow, but they always think they're cleverer than me.' Her laugh was low and sinister enough to shake the glass crystals in the chandeliers.

'I guess miracles do happen then.'

I turned over my cards one at a time to reveal a straight run from six to ten. Watching the blood boil in her cheeks was interesting. Read, Bonny, Parker, and Lamar vanished in a puff of yellow smoke. Cassie was at the table in a flash, her new blade at Lucy's throat, where it hummed with a golden hue.

I got up from my chair. 'Where's my mother?'

Cassie's knife pressed into the Devil's flesh. Lucy did nothing; no wave of the fingers to throw us to one side as she did in the hospital. Perhaps her powers couldn't work in this place.

'How did you do that? I haven't lost a game of chance in over two thousand years.'

'I counted the cards; it wasn't rocket science. Now, tell me where our mother is.'

If she didn't, Cassie would kill her; or I would.

'Your answer is inside my pocket. Can I get it without your sister cutting my throat?'

'You promised no more tricks.' It was impossible to trust her, even if we had to.

'This isn't a trick. I have what you require.'

I didn't dwell on the problem. 'One false move and Cassie will spill your blood all over this table.'

Lucy reached into her waistcoat. If she was searching for a weapon, Cassie was ready to pounce. But all she pulled out was an envelope.

'Can I tell you what's in here?'

It felt as if the endgame was on us now. 'Go ahead.'

She removed a piece of paper from the envelope; paper I recognised. Cassie gasped as Lucy read what was on it.

'We the undersigned, Alice and Cassie Arcane, solemnly swear never to harm the bearer of this document on pain of death for us and all our relatives.'

I crushed the cards in my hands as my heart threatened to stop beating, my breath coming in short staggering bursts. Cassie's hand wavered as she pulled the blade away from Lucy.

'How did you get that?' The words tumbled from my mouth.

The Devil's teeth shone brighter than the sun. 'I struck a bargain with Dracula. He got what he wanted, and I acquired this.' She held the paper up like a footballer clutching a trophy.

I dropped the cards to the floor, pushing from the chair and standing.

'Why would Dracula want our mother?' The thought of it sent a shiver through my veins.

'The self-proclaimed Lord of the Undead is, at heart, a lonely boy.' The corners of her mouth turned up as she stared into my eyes. 'He's tried living with some of his creatures, but, in reality, he detests vampires. I think it's a reflection of his self-hate. The chance to spend his torturous days with the last of the Nephilim was too much to refuse. Once my spies inside his little court told me about the pact you'd signed, I knew it would be the greatest deal I'd ever complete.'

My legs trembled, threatening to collapse. My gaze turned to Cassie, recognising the rage coursing through her face.

'What do you want?'

The Morningstar shone brightly as she answered.

'You must understand that all Michael does when faced with a problem is to meet it with brute force. He wants to end you and your sister before you become too powerful. But for me, I always look at the long game. I think you'll be useful to have around, as long as I control you. When God returns, I want the two of you on my side.'

'What happened to you saying you wanted one of us dead?'

'I changed my mind. I need all the power available to stop God from destroying my playground.'

I squashed all the confusion in my brain and processed her words.

'Does God exist?'

Lucy looked offended. She touched the side of her skull.

'I hear them in here. All the archangels do.'

'Every sentient thing hears voices in their head. Have you seen God with your own eyes?'

'The Almighty does not deem any of their creations worthy enough to gaze upon their magnificence.'

I tried to hold it in, but couldn't; I laughed like a hyena. When I stopped, she was scowling at me with enough venom to fell a giant.

'All this talk about a war between Heaven and Hell and God returning to wipe the Earth clean is because a few of you heard voices in your heads?'

The fire burned inside Lucy's eyes. Could we kill her now? But she had that contract.

And I never break my word.

The irritation drained from her face. 'Michael is crazed. We could work together to stop him.'

I moved away and ignored her. All that mattered was getting back to Whitby with Cassie and finding our mother. We pushed our way out of the pub, but Scooby didn't join us.

'How do we get out of here?' Cassie said.

I had no answer to the question as the saloon door

banged behind me. Lucy stepped outside. I was surprised to see the sadness on the Morningstar's face.

'What's the point of finding your mother if Michael will wipe her from this planet with every other living thing?'

Cassie was at my side with the knife pointed at Lucy.

'We should kill her and get this over and done with.'

'No, let's use her to leave here and look for Dracula.' I faced Lucy. 'Let's assume that God, if they exist, isn't returning home for a long time. Even with an army, does Michael have the power to erase all life from the planet?'

Lucy strode towards us, Scooby walking by her side.

'No, Michael can't do that. But humans can.'

'What do you mean?'

'For years, Michael and I used religion as a battle-ground, but for the last two centuries, we've conspired against each other in a different sphere of humanity: politics. Michael outsmarted me by using my tactics. He found a politician who appealed to people's basest desires, and now he's one devious whisper into the right ear from radioactive Armageddon flying across the planet.'

'He'll start a nuclear war?' I remembered the stories in the news about the tension in the world.

'Yes, within days, likely before you get the chance to see your mother again.'

'I thought peace talks were in progress?' I'd ignored the seriousness of the reports, too caught up in finding Mary.

'Michael has his influence in all sides, his manipulative fingers inside the White House and the British government. He won't let anybody stop this. He wants to end all human life before the Almighty returns. We need to stop him before it's too late.'

'How do we do that?' Cassie tried to control her anger

and failed, her cheeks transforming into a delicate shade of purple.

Lucy's eyes sparkled yellow. 'You'll do it with my help.'

I dragged my sister to the side, beyond the empty tables where some of the worst of humanity had sat not so long ago. Cassie's eyes were on fire.

'We should kill her now, take Scooby, and then search for Dracula.'

I liked the sound of all that, but knew we couldn't do it.

'She has the contract we signed, Cassie. We can't kill her.'

She beat a fist into her palm. 'Who cares about that piece of paper? Nobody will know what we've done.' The knife given to her by Brigid the Smith shimmered with a yellow hue. 'I bet that's why those women gave me this, because it's a Devil-killing blade.'

As I considered her words, I noticed the same shimmering coming from my pocket. I removed the book Brigid the Poet had handed to me and opened it. The first page wasn't blank anymore, containing a single sentence: *honour your promises.*

I showed it to Cassie. 'I never break my word, Sister.'

She shook her head. 'So, where does that leave us?'

I glanced over Cassie's shoulder at Lucy fiddling with her phone.

'We work with her until we get what we want.'

Cassie let out a long sigh. 'You know we can't trust her.'

'Of course, and we'll be on our guard for that, and that's why we'll be the ones using her. Do you agree?'

She nodded. It took a minute of whispered conversation between us before we settled on a plan. Then I spoke to Lucy.

'We'll work together with you to stop Michael, but once it's over, all bets are off, and you'll tear up that contract.'

'And you'll help us find our mother,' Cassie added.

Lucy performed an extravagant bow and beamed at us.

'I agree to your terms, Children of the Arcane.'

With a click of her fingers, we vanished and reappeared on a bridge. I stared across at the Houses of Parliament, the smell of the Thames filling my lungs.

And then I bent over and threw up.

I couldn't remember the last time I'd eaten, maybe at Vika's party, but whatever it was came thundering out of my mouth and into the river.

Cassie put a hand on my shoulder as my guts grumbled like thunder.

'Are you okay, Alice?'

I wiped vomit from my lips and lifted up. 'I'll survive.'

'I'm sorry, girls, I didn't think instantaneous teleportation would harm you.'

'I'm fine,' Cassie said.

I scowled at her. 'Well, bully for you, Sister.' I glanced across the river, wondering why we were in London, but there were more pressing questions. 'Why do you need us in this battle with Michael? What can we do that an archangel can't?'

All this time in the supernatural world, I'd struggled because I felt science could answer everything, but I was fooling myself, which left me uninformed about the new sphere I travelled in. I needed more information, and even though she was untrustworthy, I knew Lucy would be the best person to get answers from to the questions which had accumulated in my head since the werewolf attacked me in Middlesbrough.

People moved around us, the traffic going in every direction. We were invisible to them as they passed by without a glance or a word. Lucy crossed to a wall and sat on it.

'My brother has manipulated humanity, so it finds itself squabbling over territory in Asia. It's not the first time he's done this, but it will be the most serious if this gets out of hand. The American President and the British Prime Minister have gathered their war cabinets in secret locations in their respective countries; secret to most but me. It's in these two places he'll use his influence to set Armageddon in motion. I need to get inside both locations to stop this, but he's warded both places against me. He's also collected a legion of witches and warlocks to create a mystical barrier behind an army of angels, demons and monsters. There is only so far I can go before Michael knows of my presence, but he can't detect you two because of your unique biology.'

'Even if we could get into these protected compounds, how are we supposed to deal with the security?' Cassie voiced my doubts.

'I'll train you in your natural abilities, and then you decide which location you want to travel to.'

'We won't go together, one place at a time?' I said.

'This will only work if the attacks are synchronised: one of you in the UK, the other in the US.'

'What do you mean by natural abilities?' Cassie said.

'You and your sister are both human and the Divine, a bloodline collected of talents yet to be discovered, but some things will come to you as you get older: you are the Arcane. I can quicken the process and help you hone your skills now when you need them the most, because without your strengths, it will be impossible to defeat Michael and his forces.'

'You expect me to believe that the Devil, the Queen of Lies, needs to save the world while the archangel Michael wants to destroy it? Weren't you cast out of Heaven because of your jealousy of humanity, so you've spent your banishment making humans suffer?' How could I trust her?

'You don't know the true story of my banishment, child, but there'll be no one left to torture if you're extinct; no more wonderful, shabby humans to bargain with.' Lucy appeared to be losing her temper. 'A lifeless world is of no use to me, and even less to you. What's the point of you reuniting with your mother if you'll all be dead soon after?' A fiery redness consumed her eyes. 'So, do you want me to train you or not?'

I looked at Cassie as she stared at me, knowing we had little choice in the matter.

'Okay. Where do we begin?' I said.

Lucy's smile was like an exploding star. And I was getting sunburnt.

'We have little time before Michael will act, so I can only teach you the basics of what you'll master one day. We'll start with invisibility.' Lucy vanished after she finished speaking. 'Do you see me?' Her voice hovered in the air, her body nowhere in sight.

'No,' Cassie and I said together.

'Good.' Lucy reappeared, floating ten inches above the grass. 'Then we have levitation.'

'Cool,' Cassie said.

I expected the public to swarm over us in startled surprise, but everyone continued to go about their business, oblivious to the wonders in their midst.

'That's followed by teleportation.' She disappeared, and then returned behind us, six feet from the ground. 'Last, we have the most difficult combination: telekinesis.' She pointed her hand at me and pulled me through the air so I floated close to her face. 'And telepathy.' Her lips didn't move, her voice crawling around inside my skull. It was an unpleasant sensation, much like I'd imagine it would feel to have a slug slithering over your brain, with its slimy trail stinging every part.

Can you hear me, Alice?

I wobbled my head, trying to throw her out, and she dropped me to the floor. I landed with a bump, legs giving out under me as I sat on the ground.

'How can we do these miracles?' Cassie helped me up, her voice full of doubt, and I shared the impossibility of doing what Lucy showed us.

'You'll do these and more. The power lies in your blood, in your specific DNA, but the actualisation rests in your mind. Believe you will do these things, believe in yourself, and then you will.'

Cassie appeared keen to try, but I had my suspicions.

'I have difficulty getting out of bed some days, so how can I do what you did?'

'Take my hand and I'll give you a boost.' Lucy held her arms out wide as if waiting to be pressed against an invisible crucifix. Cassie took her right hand, but I hesitated. What if this was all a trap?

'Come on, Alice,' said my sister.

I clasped Lucy's left hand and waited.

'Okay, girls; we'll start with levitation.' She stared straight ahead. 'Feel the difference inside you, reach down and find that connection to your ancestors from thousands of years ago. Then imagine you're stepping off the ground and into the air. Move up and float.'

I did as she said, closing my eyes and focusing on the beating of my heart. My mind drifted down from my head, through my veins and swam into the centre of my being. I searched and searched, but there were no images of my ancestors, only a blurred sight of a hospital bed. Even then, I couldn't see the face of my mother.

My blood was still as I squeezed Lucy's hand and tried again, and again. But there was nothing. I wrenched from her in frustration, turning to Cassie to blurt out my disappointment, but it caught in my throat as she floated up. I watched her rise. It was impossible, but it kept happening and happening; she lifted six inches from the ground, and then more until her feet were level with Lucy's shoulder. For one second, I thought she might glide away until Lucy pulled her back.

Cassie landed and yelped. 'That was amazing.'

'Just be careful your attention doesn't waver, or you could drift into the clouds and never get down again.'

'I couldn't do it,' I said.

Cassie tried it again, steadying herself a foot above the ground. My chest was heavy as she grinned at me and walked on air above the grass before lifting to cross over a group of rose bushes. Bees flew from the flowers and hovered around her legs.

Lucy turned to me. 'Don't worry; it'll come to you.'

'What's next?' Cassie's eyes bulged, appearing unable to contain her excitement as she re-joined us on the ground.

'Let's try invisibility,' Lucy replied. 'Focus your mind on the perception you have of yourself, the image you have of your body, then wipe it from your thoughts so in its place is only nothing.'

I assumed this would be easy, considering the times I'd viewed myself as nothing and watched people stare right through me. My eyes were open this time, focusing on the trees ahead and picturing myself disappearing inside the greenery. I visualised myself as a slice of nature vanishing into zero, thought of my legs and arms as one gigantic whole blending into the background like a chameleon.

The swarm of bees continued to linger near Cassie, and as I watched them to make sure they wouldn't attack her, I noticed the grass near her legs was full of crawling insects. Was this something to do with us looking for the powers we weren't supposed to have until we were older? I puzzled over that idea as I continued to focus on myself as nothing, to imagine those bees flying straight for me because they didn't know I was there.

I got the same results as with the levitation, staring at my hands as they trembled. As nothing happened to me, I watched as Cassie disappeared from existence bit by bit. It was strange to see her face vanish, and then her torso, so only her fingers lingered in the air until they went; the last thing I saw of her was Cassie waving at me. Then she went poof into nothingness. The bees must have been as confused as me as they flew away and disappeared into the trees. The insects in the grass followed them, and I wondered if my sister hadn't turned herself invisible, but had vanished into another dimension.

'I can't see my arms.' Her voice came from a void. 'And I can fly.' I couldn't see her, but she was above my head, tickling at my ear.

I flinched backwards and hid my annoyance. 'How do you feel?'

Her laugh irritated me more than I thought it would. 'I'm on top of the world, Sis.'

'Come down and show yourself,' Lucy said.

Cassie did as instructed, popping out of nowhere to land next to me. She was the happiest I'd seen her since we'd met across a dead werewolf in the park.

Lucy Morningstar, our deadliest enemy less than an

hour ago, now had the face of a concerned mother. The thought of it turned my guts into a whirlpool.

'Ensure you don't hang on to these gifts for too long.'

'What would happen if we did?' I wasn't sure why I was worried as they weren't working for me.

'These powers are things your bodies are years away from being able to deal with. I'm only teaching you them because of the desperate situation we're in. If you hold on to them longer than necessary, you might not return. You could levitate into the clouds and never get back, turn invisible and stay like that forever, or teleport into solid matter and die.'

'We'll be fine,' Cassie said as she disappeared, then appeared on the other side of me, and then in front of Lucy. 'This will save on using planes, and think how good it'll be for the environment. I can go to Paris and Rome in an instant now.' She was enjoying herself too much for my liking.

'At your age, you're only able to teleport to places you can see,' Lucy said.

Cassie hopped in and out of view like an overexcited jack-in-the-box. I squeezed my mind and got zilch.

'Nothing's working for me.'

Lucy put her hand on my arm, her fingers feeling warm outside my clothes.

'To be honest, I didn't expect it to work so quickly for either of you. Perhaps this is all too early for you, and Cassie is a natural because she has more experience with the supernatural.'

I watched my sister bounce around like a demented rabbit until she landed in front of me.

'Even with everything you've seen and done since we

met, your science brain won't let go of what you perceive to be logic and reason. You need to relax more.'

I'm sure she didn't mean to sound condescending, but she did. Perhaps she was right, maybe they both were, but how could I unwind when the fate of the world was in my hands?

'Your physical bond could help,' Lucy said. 'Reach into your sister's mind, Cassie, and speak to her without moving your lips.'

It wasn't like a slug worming its way into my brain this time, more of a gentle caress from tender fingers.

Can you hear me, Alice?

Yes.

I hear you too. See, you can do it.

But why couldn't I do the other things like you did?

I'm unsure, Alice. Maybe Lucy is right, and it'll take time.

I don't trust her.

Me neither, but we'll use her for what we need, sort out this problem with Michael, and then deal with her.

I still blame her for Mother's abduction.

So do I. But once this is over, we'll make her take us to Dracula, and we'll rescue Mother from him. Lucy teaching us how to use these abilities will backfire on her because we'll end up being stronger than her.

You might, but I won't.

As Cassie reached into my mind, it was like she'd put a hand on my arm to console me. I could feel her fingers on my skin even though she was two feet away from me.

Try and relax, Alice, and then it will come. I'm sure of it.

'If you girls are finished, we have to move on.' Lucy's voice brought us back into the real world.

'How come that worked for me, but the other things didn't?' I asked her.

Lucy frowned and scratched her head. 'I'm not all-knowing, but your sibling connection might have allowed the telepathy to work for you. Why don't you attempt it with me?'

The thought of it made me shiver. 'No, let's stick with the telekinesis.'

Lucy pointed behind me. 'Okay. Focus on that rock and try to lift it with your mind.'

I stared at the piece of rubble twenty feet away. I wasn't sure what to do, squeezing my eyes and glaring at it. I dug my nails into my palms and tried again, holding my breath and studying the stone. I imagined stretching my arm out like a rubber band and lifting the rock, clasping it in my hand and throwing it into the air. Nothing happened, and I gave up in frustration. As I did so, it rose from the ground and floated towards Cassie, who caught it in her hand. She grinned so much, I thought she might bite into it as if it was an apple.

'Strike four out of five for me,' I said.

Lucy watched me, something dazzling behind her gaze.

'I'll stay in the UK with you, and Cassie will handle the US.'

I glared at her, tension rushing through my shoulders.

'I thought you said Michael would know if you were there?'

Her eyes narrowed and sparkled at the same time. 'We'll use that to our advantage, as a distraction, especially since you're not ready to develop your potential just yet. It's the same with all children: some mature quicker than others. Perhaps your mother plopped Cassie out first.'

Cassie pushed past the Queen of Lies before I punched

the Devil on the nose. Lucy grinned and strode across the road and on to the grass.

'Ignore her, Alice. She's only trying to wind you up.'

My head was like a kettle, ready to boil. 'She's doing a good job.'

Cassie pulled me to one side. 'Whatever her motives, at least she's given us another way of communicating with each other, and I've got a few more tricks up my sleeve.'

I know she didn't intend me to feel bad about it, but I did.

'It's stupid,' I said. 'I should be happy for you, not feeling sorry for myself.'

'I think this is because I've been immersed in this world for years now, while it's still new for you. Just give it time.'

She was right, but I didn't feel any better. I hugged her, then let go.

'What's the plan?'

'Let's ask our partner,' Cassie said as we strode hand in hand across the road. The original fallen angel sat on the grass, making a daisy chain necklace.

'We should all wear one of these and give ourselves a super team name; how about Lucy and the Twins? Or Lucy and the Arcane?'

I tried my best to push my failures to the side. 'Now you've taught us new tricks, how do we stop Michael from starting a nuclear war?'

Lucy threw the garlands in the air. 'I'm glad you asked. My dear brother has been splitting himself into two for the last few years, spending his time possessing the White House Secretary of State and the British Foreign Secretary, guiding and influencing the foreign policy of both countries. He's also manipulated the populations of those nations so they have leaders who are rabid warmongers. He's got them ready to push the nuclear button on many imagined enemies. You must clear the way for me to get in there to set them straight.'

I laughed in her face. 'You're asking us to trust the Devil to save the world?'

Lucy caught one of the flower necklaces and dropped it over her head.

'Don't believe everything you've heard about me. I told you, I need humans around; what would I do without them?'

'How do we get to the leaders?' Cassie said.

Lucy sprang to her feet, smelling of roses. 'My forces are outside both locations pretending to be peaceful protesters. They'll cause a disturbance with the security, Michael's supernatural army. Then you'll teleport as close as you can to the main building.'

I spotted the first flaw in the plan. 'We've already determined I can't do that.'

'And that's why I'll take you there.'

'Won't that alert Michael to your presence?'

'Yes, but it means he'll have to confront me, leaving the US base weaker and more open to Cassie. While I'm busy with him in the UK, Alice will complete her mission.'

'Which is what?'

'Each of you has to locate the leader of the country you're in and break them free of Michael's influence, restore normality to their minds, and defuse the threat of war.'

'How do we do that?'

'You'll figure it out when you find them, but you must do it, whatever the cost.'

I stared at Lucy. 'What does that mean?'

Her eyes sank into mine. 'The fate of billions rests in your hands, Children of the Nephilim. If you don't stop this no matter what, then untold innocents will die because of you.'

Cassie laughed. 'You can't guilt-trip me, Lucy. I'll kill whoever I need to for this.' She looked at me. 'I'm sure Alice will do the same if she has to.'

I didn't acknowledge that and focused on Lucy. 'And then what happens?'

'The three of us will join together to imprison Michael in the Cage.'

'What cage?'

'It's where God imprisoned me so long ago. It exists in the abyss which separates Heaven and Hell.'

It was more information to overwhelm me; my brain was like mincemeat in a frying pan. The only way I'd survive this was to treat it like a mathematical puzzle.

'When do we start?' I said.

'No time like the present.' Lucy grabbed our hands, and we disappeared.

We landed in a splodge of mud in an English field, just Lucy and me. Crazed butterflies beat their wings against my ribs, and the air stank of gasoline. I bent over and vomited, my throat straining against the bile. Then I wiped my mouth and glared at her.

'Where's Cassie?' I thought Lucy's foolish plan had already derailed.

'I've dropped her off in the States.' Lucy strode down the hill. 'I could have gotten nearer than this, but we shouldn't announce my arrival to Michael until the last minute. Can you see the crowd ahead?'

I nodded. A few hundred yards away was a swarm of people hoisting protest placards. I didn't want to be there, worried about Cassie. As we got closer, I saw the fence beyond the protesters and the row of uniformed police officers guarding it. Behind them was a magnificent building, a stately home that might have belonged to the Royal Family.

The wind whistled through my hair as I ignored the growing noise from the crowd below us and turned to my guide.

'You said Michael has been planning this for a long time, manipulating politicians into a nuclear war.' The Devil peered at me through feminine eyes, and it created an itch on my back that I couldn't reach. 'So he caused the conflict in the South China Sea?'

Lucy nodded. 'Contrary to popular myth, my brother is the arch manipulator in the family, not me. He also has a great ability to predict future events years in advance. All he needed to do was move the human pieces around like on a chessboard.'

'And he did this in Asia?'

'China has long regarded Taiwan as a province that must be reunited with the mainland, by force if necessary. In recent months, China sent twenty-five warplanes through the island's airspace, the largest reported incursion to date, and had an aircraft carrier lead a large naval exercise near Taiwan. To counter all of this, Taiwan continued with its secret nuclear weapons programme; only it wasn't so secret.'

'Michael made sure the Chinese government knew what was happening in Taiwan?'

'He did. And he also manoeuvred the sinking of the American warship in the area. Once you combine all those factors with his manipulation of the American and British leaders, it can only lead to one thing.'

I interrupted her. 'If both of you can time travel, surely you know what the future holds?'

She waved a finger at me. 'Travelling through time is a dangerous and unpredictable venture, only to be attempted as a last resort. Like you and Cassie did to find your mother.'

'And look where that got us.' The irony wasn't lost on me.

'Indeed. We might not be standing here if you hadn't taken that risk.'

'So you and Michael know what happens in the future?'

Lucy shook her head. 'No, I'm afraid not. As a budding scientist, I'm sure you know the universe is composed of energy: dark energy, dark matter, ordinary matter, electromagnetic radiation and antimatter. That includes not only living things and places, but time.' I had a sudden vision of the Devil teaching a science class at university. 'And through time, there are bursts of energy which cannot be travelled to or passed through, such as the beginning and end of everything. And today is one of these times. Neither Michael nor I can travel beyond this point.'

The implication being a large burst of energy was imminent: thousands of nuclear weapons raging destruction across the planet. Maybe I hadn't considered the possibility before because it appeared so remote. And my obsession with finding my mother was the only thing that concerned me. But now, it seemed all too real.

'How long have we got?'

Lucy handed me a watch. 'Put this on. You have an hour to stop the end of the world.'

I did as she said, slipping the digital timepiece over my wrist. The numbers looked to be moving faster than my heartbeat. I peered at the crowd ahead of us, surprised by one omission.

'There are no cameras or media.'

She gazed down at them.

'This isn't a conflict the planet needs to witness, Alice. Even on the verge of Armageddon, some things are best kept hidden.'

We reached the bottom of the hill and the few hundred activists there. Only they weren't activists as I recognised werewolves next to demons, angels next to ghouls. They all stopped moving when they saw Lucy. She communicated to them in their heads. I couldn't hear what she said, but the buzzing at the front of my brain like vigorous wasps told me something was going on.

They turned away and marched towards the police and the flimsy fence separating them.

'What did you tell them?'

'I instructed them to be good little soldiers and sacrifice themselves for their Queen.'

They moved forward like it was a military operation, and I glanced at Lucy. Was any of what she told me true? Was her brother, the archangel Michael, the true architect of the madness playing out around me?

She grinned as her soldiers went to war. I watched as they charged the line and burst through the fence. The things masquerading as police removed their weapons and fired, with a volley of bullets hitting the front row of Lucy's soldiers. It was carnage, but her loyal followers threw themselves forward, stepping over their fallen colleagues and crashing into the security. The noise engulfed me, of vampires screaming, werewolves howling, and demons roaring their calls to death. In less than a minute, the heaving mass was nothing but blood and bones seeping into the English countryside, turning green into red as the bodies piled up. It should have horrified me, but there was a fascination in the violence which worried me.

I glanced away from the slaughter to look at Lucy, but she'd already forgotten about them.

'We need to be inside that mansion, but the mystical barrier is strong. I can get us outside, and then it's up to you. Are you ready?'

Before I could reply, she grabbed my hand and we

vanished. Thick cotton wool buds soaked in bleach appeared to fill my head as we reappeared at the back of the building, hidden behind the first hedge of a vast garden maze. I tumbled into it and threw up. Then I grabbed my stomach and scowled at her.

'You could have warned me.'

She smiled and shrugged. 'The protection deflected us to the rear of the mansion, but it will have been like a bomb exploding for Michael. He'll recall his essence from America and be here soon. You need to get to that door and inside.' She pointed to the entrance. 'Can you do that, Alice?'

I pushed through the bushes without replying; there was the taste of stale food in my mouth and stabbing pain in my guts. Two people stood outside the building. If I tried to analyse how irrational this plan was, I knew I wouldn't do it; so I ran to them. I affected my best-panicked voice and screamed, but the pain flowing through me was real.

The men held on to tridents as if guarding the gates of Atlantis, baring their teeth and purple eyes before aiming their weapons at me. Demon voices slithered from their mouths.

'What are you doing here, child?'

'I was attacked in the woods.' I wiped an invisible tear from my cheek. 'Can you help me?'

The taller one grinned at me, a startling look straight from a cannibal's cookbook.

'Nothing can help you now, girl.' He placed his trident to the side and reached for me.

I stumbled back and searched for the hidden Arcane strength inside me, but found nothing but frustration and annoyance. The other demon was unmoving.

'Leave the child alone, Moloch. If you leave your post, Michael will roast you over the pit for an eternity.'

Moloch snarled at him. 'Why did we flee Hell if it was only to supplicate ourselves at his feet? The She-Devil is ruthless, but he's insane.'

I waited for them to argue, hoping it would allow me to slip past them and inside.

'We go where the power is, brother, and that's not with the Morningstar now. She's as weak and desperate as this child.' He peered at me as if I was a Big Mac during a half-price sale. 'Now kill the girl so we can go back to work.'

Tension rippled through my legs as I readied for them to attack, only to be distracted as a shadow dropped from the sky to land inside the maze. The demons saw it too. Fear and respect gripped their faces as they raised their hands to their eyes, but it was too late. An enormous explosion followed a blinding flash of light.

The blast threw me through the air, arm across my head as my shoulder thudded into a guard. We kept on going backwards and smashing through the door. The demon's body engulfed me, and it was that which saved my life. The force of the boom split the monster's body apart as his grip cocooned me. His arms fell from me, followed by his legs, and head separating from the shoulders and rolling to the side. Then the other demon was hurled through the entrance and smashed into the hallway table.

Blood and bone surrounded me, sticking to my arms and legs as the infernal ringing of a thousand bells invaded my ears. Splintered wood hovered in the air, mixed in with shattered organs and the smell of burnt flesh. I grabbed my throat before I threw up again.

I lifted in slow motion, limbs aching and fit to burst. There was a huge gap where the doors should have been.

Through it, I saw a blaze of light smashing against more of the same. I had to shield my eyes and peer at it through trembling fingers. Was this the form archangels took when they fought each other?

Lucy had promised a distraction, and here it was; only I was in no shape to use it. I wanted to curl up and go to sleep. Perhaps I could dream about being back at university. I lay amongst the rubble of timber and skin and closed my eyes, but all that appeared were images of those who'd suffered since I'd stepped into this world: Akemi, my neighbours, Sarda, all those in Limbo and Purgatory, the prisoners of the Collectors; and most of all, my mother.

'Are you okay, dear?'

I opened my eyes to see two women standing over me. They held out their hands and grabbed me. As I got up, warm liquid slid down my forehead and across my cheek.

'We need to get that cut looked at,' one woman said.

'Dr Weaver is downstairs,' the other replied.

'Will they let us into the bunker?' the first woman said.

'They must,' the other replied. 'This child is hardly a terrorist, is she?'

They marched me away from the debris and into a lift. Not once did they look at the cacophony of light exploding outside; it was as if they didn't know it was there.

'What's your name, dear?' one of them asked me as we descended inside the metal box.

'It's Alice,' I said.

They laughed together. 'Well, Alice, you're heading down the rabbit hole now.'

I focused my mind and tried to reach into theirs, using the power of telepathy Lucy had taught me. All I got was blank stares and one of them scratching at her temple.

'Oh, there was a spasm in my head there. I hope I don't have a migraine coming on.'

'Well, we are going to the doctor,' the other said as the lift opened and we stepped out. In front of us were another door and more armed guards. These two appeared normal, not demons in human form.

'We need to be inside, boys,' one woman said to a guard.

'Authorised personnel only,' he replied.

'Can't you see this poor girl's injured?' she said.

'And I've got a screaming headache, ya daft bastard,' said the other.

Only her lips never moved and I heard her in my mind. It had worked, after all!

I gazed at the security and tried it on him.

Look at the girl. She has authorised clearance. You've allowed her in before; you know you have.

I repeated it again and again, staring right into his eyes.

Then I felt the switch click inside his head.

'Of course, Ministers. I'll let you all in.' He moved to the side and opened the door.

It was a hive of activity in the bunker. There must have been twenty people buzzing about, not including us, and a plethora of active digital screens of all sizes. Most prominent of all was the giant board at the back, which took up the entire wall. It was split into two, one half showing an electronic map of the UK, the other displaying the rest of the world. The outline of China glowed red.

The women led me to a comfy sofa and sat me in it.

'You stay here, dear, and we'll find Dr Weaver for you.'
Once she's sorted this banging headache out for me.

I heard her again inside my head as she walked away. As I tried to come to terms with my new ability, the other woman brought a tall, grey-haired man to me. He was distinguished and handsome, with a smile bright enough to light up the room. He held out his hand, and I recognised him immediately.

'Pleased to meet you, Alice,' he said as I shook hands with the Prime Minister of the United Kingdom.

This was the person I'd come here to cure or kill.

22 CASSIE

I'm Cassie Arcane and I was born to kill monsters. I'd only discovered my real name and heritage days ago, but here I was, standing in front of hundreds of fiends I'd promised to destroy. This is what I loved to do. These creatures stared at me, these supernatural beasts, glaring at the assassin Lucy had left with them: a collection of vampires, werewolves, trolls, demons, and the rest.

Would they attack or help me?

I reached for the blade in my pocket as the horde parted and one of them strode towards me. She was small and thin and looked younger than me. She had dirty blonde hair cut to her shoulders, was wearing an immaculate Armani suit. This girl moved as if she was the ruler of the world and wanted everyone to know it. She had the unmistakable darkness of the undead.

As she stood before me, the penetrating blue of her eyes and the whiteness of her vampire teeth dazzled me. She smiled and bowed with a flourish.

'Welcome, Cassandra Arcane, Leader of the Queen of

Hell's Legion. My name is Claudia and I am yours to command.'

A puff of wind could have knocked me over at that moment.

'I'm in charge of these... these...'

'Warriors?' Her voice was young and soulful, her eyes burning with ancient wisdom.

'Monsters,' I replied.

'Monsters are what we need to get through Michael's hordes, my commander.'

'Why can't I teleport into the building?' She'd called me commander, but it felt like she was the one in charge.

'Your Arcane powers are in their nascent stage, Cassie. That hellhole is too far away for you to make a single jump, and a series of short ones will only announce your arrival sooner than we want. I have to guide you inside.'

'Why do I need you to guide me in there?' I glanced over the horde. 'I can lead these monsters into battle.'

Claudia nodded at me. 'That is undoubtedly true, commander, but you require someone who knows the layout of the building to navigate your way inside, and nobody has more experience than me.'

'You've lived in there?'

Claudia flashed those sparkling fangs again. 'I suffered and died in that place; me and many others. I could never call it living. My true life started when I was reborn.'

I didn't know what to say, unable to process what horrors she must have endured. Yet she stood before me, a vampire, a creature I'd sworn to kill. Then I remembered how Bella and Vika had helped Alice and me.

'What do we do?' I said.

Claudia removed a phone bigger than her hand from her pocket.

'Everything has to phase with events in Britain with your sister. The President and your Prime Minister, manipulated and controlled by Michael, have fixed a time for their joint nuclear launch, and this is the countdown.'

She showed me the screen: it was set for one hour away.

'That doesn't give us a lot of time,' I said.

'And that's why we start now.'

She took my hand and I didn't resist; her skin was warm, and it surprised me. She walked me through Lucy's troops – my troops now – and towards the combat-clad guards pointing their shields our way. To the world, they would appear to be police mixed in with soldiers, but I guessed they were something more than that.

Claudia let go of my hand. 'We need you to scatter an opening through them, My Lady Arcane.'

There must have been two hundred of them staring at me. 'And how do I do that?'

She tapped her skull. 'Use your mind, My Lady.'

A growl of anticipation grew behind me, my troops readying for action. I gazed at the enemy and then ran, sprinting forward with only one image in my head: giant hands prising them apart and tossing them left and right. I was fifty yards from them and nothing was happening. Their fiery red eyes screamed at me as I approached.

Thirty yards and they were unmoving.

If this all went wrong, I was toast.

Twenty yards and I could smell their hate.

Ten yards and shields and batons came for my head.

I was in their faces when they flew left and right like petals in a hurricane. Dozens of them scattered before me, arms and legs splitting apart as my mind tore into them. Power surged through my veins, and it was euphoric.

A roar erupted behind me, followed by the sound of

thunderous feet. When I stopped and turned, I was through the gap and a furious battle was underway.

Then Claudia was by my side. 'That was excellent, My Lady Cassandra. Now we head for the building.' There was no time to observe the clash behind us.

'Call me Cassie,' I said as we ran together. Her presence reminded me of Alice, and I wondered how she'd fared in her challenge across the ocean.

As I thought about my sister, something substantial dropped from the sky and onto my back. Claws dug into my flesh and pushed me to the ground.

'Harpies,' Claudia shouted as another attacked her.

The beast gripped my jacket and lifted me in the air. It screeched into my face as we rose. Below me, the battle raged on, wind swirling through my hair as panic threatened to consume me. I grappled with the creature's legs, clutching at gnarled skin. These were stronger than the ones we'd fought in Limbo. Its sharp teeth were snapping at my fingers before I remembered what Lucy had taught me.

I teleported two feet from its grasp, levitating as its fangs bit into emptiness. Before it reacted, I flew towards the beast and plunged my knife deep into its neck. It struggled to scream as blood gushed from the wound. I removed the blade and watched the harpy plunge to its death.

I floated for a second before following the monster, aiming for its sister pinning Claudia to the ground. I got there before the dead thing hit the grass, my arm wrenching the harpy's head back and throwing it off the vampire. It was up in a flash, but I was ready for it, teleporting to the side and slashing its face as it went by. As it turned, Claudia was on it. She sank her teeth into its throat, biting down so hard, she severed its head from its shoulders in one go. She tossed its body into the dirt and wiped the blood from her chin.

'We make a good team, Cassie Arcane.'

I couldn't reply, legs buckling under me as I sat down. Clouds of dizziness seeped through my brain.

'I feel sick.' My guts churned, my neck jerking to the side as I threw up next to the dead harpy. My throat was on fire, the air filled with the stink of death. I looked at my hand and it blurred into a ghostly shape.

Claudia took my arm. 'You used too many powers too soon; you've drained your stamina and your stability.'

I didn't argue with her, wanting to lie down and sleep.

'How much time do we have?'

She showed me the countdown on her phone: fifty minutes. Behind us were the screams of the dying. Claudia offered me her hand.

'We have to go now, Cassie.'

I grabbed her fingers and she lifted me. We moved forward at a slow jog, all the time checking the sky for more threats. My legs wobbled like jelly; my senses overwhelmed me. The mansion was only two minutes away. My vision was hazy, so I couldn't make out what was in front of the building, but I guessed it wouldn't be unguarded.

I seized hold of Claudia's arm and we stopped running. I was glad for the breather.

'Shouldn't we have a plan?' I said.

Claudia stared at me with startled eyes. 'Didn't the Queen of Hell tell you what she wanted?'

My breathing came in shallow bursts, but most of the fog lifted from my brain.

'She told me to either force the President to come to his senses or kill him. There were no details of how to get in, get past the security, or how to change his mind.'

The vampire grinned. 'The first two are my responsibility; the last one, you're on your own with. Unless you want me to help you slay him?'

A thousand tiny insects buzzed at the insides of my skull.

'No, that's an extreme last resort. How are you going to achieve the first two?'

'Can you see the security at the front?'

I had a clear view, staring at a dozen armed guards. 'Are any of them human?'

'I expect so. Even if you were feeling a hundred per cent, you couldn't teleport past them because you don't know the layout inside the building. You could turn invisible, but I doubt you can hold that form for too long in your present condition.'

'What about flying up to a window and entering like that?'

Claudia wrinkled her eyebrows at me. 'You've still got the problem of your powers possibly failing you at the worst time, plus some guards are bound to see you in the air. No, we have to find another entrance.'

'And how do we do that?'

'Follow me.' She scampered off to the clump of trees on our right. There couldn't have been more than forty minutes left. Birds scattered before us, and a gust of wind brushed the fog from my brain as strength returned to my bones while euphoria flashed through my senses.

When I reached the edge of the forest, Claudia had disappeared, vanished as if she'd never existed. Branches shook as leaves swirled across my feet. Had this been a trap all along? A squirrel jumped through the trees; the blade was in my hand before it landed on the bark next to me. It scratched its nose and stared at me before scampering up and out of sight.

'You're twitchy, aren't you?'

I spun around, arm outstretched and knife pointing forward, to find Claudia grinning at me.

'You disappeared.' I made it sound like an accusation.

'I had to make sure the entrance was still here.' She stepped to the side, her feet kicking away the bunch of leaves covering the ground.

'The entrance to what?'

'Technically, I suppose it's more of an exit.' She finished sweeping with her foot to reveal a dirty wooden hatch. She crouched down and opened it.

'This is the tunnel slaves used to escape into the forest.' Her eyes misted over and the shudder in her voice was unmistakable.

'But not you?'

She sucked in her chest and let out a massive breath of air. I'd assumed vampires didn't need to breathe, so it was a surprise to me.

'No, not me.' That was all she said, and I didn't push her. 'Shall we?' She stepped into the tunnel.

I followed, finding the steps chiselled into the dirt. There was nothing but darkness and the smell of the earth as I climbed down. When I reached the bottom, Claudia was standing there with the torch shining from her phone. I removed mine and did the same. I stuck to her heels as she moved forward, an aroma of damp mud clinging to my lungs.

'Where does this lead?' I dodged the rats scurrying at my feet. All the warmth had been sucked away and I zipped up my jacket against the chill.

'There's a compound at the back where they chained

me and the others. It's something much more respectable now, so we should come out at the rear end of the stables. The original entrance was sealed a century ago, but it was reinstated recently.'

We crept forward as quickly as we could without falling over. 'Why was that?'

'Vampires and other creatures are trafficked through this part of the US.'

The air turned colder. 'Trafficked by whom and why?'

'There's so much you don't know, Cassie Arcane, about what you've killed.'

I put my hand on her shoulder and we stopped. 'Then tell me.'

It was a tight spot, but she twisted her head to me. 'Not everything is black and white, Cassie. Good and bad exist in the supernatural world just as they do in the human one. Surely you've realised this by now?'

I thought about the Nexus and what went on there; of Kai, Bella and Vika; of Scooby the Hellhound; of the Gorgon who Alice befriended; of the Collectors and their prisoners, and the creatures above us fighting to save humanity.

'So who is enslaving vampires and the others?'

'The people who invented slavery: humans.' Before I could reply, she turned and shone her torch on to the steps leading up. 'We're here,' she said as she climbed.

Claudia lifted the hatch off effortlessly. She scrambled out, and I followed her into a dank but empty stable. The smell of horses was everywhere, but I couldn't see any.

'How much time do we have?'

'Thirty minutes,' she replied.

The back of the house was only a few yards away. There were no guards, which was suspicious. Claudia held her finger to her lips as six giants strode into view, all of them at least ten feet tall, scanning their surroundings through a single eye in the middle of their foreheads.

Claudia whispered in my ear, 'Trust Michael to be that arrogant and use a squad of cyclops as security.'

They were stationed outside the back doors. There was no way past them without a battle, a fight we had no chance of winning.

'What now?' I said.

'Do you feel up to using your powers again?'

My body ached with a constant buzz at the rear of my skull, but I couldn't tell her that.

'Absolutely.'

'Okay. Do you see the open window at the top of the mansion?' She pointed to the roof. I nodded. 'We'll fly up there and go in through it.'

My eyes narrowed in amazement. 'Don't take this the wrong way, but I doubt I can carry you up there.'

She shook her head and grinned at me. 'You know vampires can fly, right?'

'I didn't know that.'

'Well, now you do.' She bent to pick up a barrel of hay. It was large enough to take two men to carry, but she grabbed it in one small, delicate hand. She crept towards the front of the barn, both of us only yards away from the cyclops guards.

'What next?' I said.

'I'll use this to distract them. As soon as they turn, we fly to that window. Understood?'

'Yes.'

Claudia yanked her arm back and hefted the barrel into the air. It landed with a tumultuous noise twenty feet to our right, bouncing off a wall and splitting apart. Six solitary eyes turned in that direction. In that instant, Claudia and I lifted together, her arms around me as she held on tight. We sped through the air, landing on the roof in a blink of an eye. In the blink of six eyes, even.

My heart pounded as we climbed through the window. The room was empty, filled with children's toys and mountains of books. Dust was everywhere and I stopped myself from sneezing. The motion made me think of Scooby; I missed the shaggy Hellhound.

'This was the nursery.' Claudia walked to the door. She didn't open it, putting her head close to the wood and listening. After a minute, she returned to me.

'There are two floors below this and a basement. The President is in there with his war cabinet. We've got twenty minutes left, and there are forty guards between us and them, all of which are demons in human form. A dozen we could take, but not that many, not in the time we have. So there's only one choice remaining.'

'Which is?'

She took my hand and we sat on two plastic chairs shaped as pink dragons.

'I'll cause a commotion outside and keep the security busy.'

'That sounds like suicide to me.' I was concerned about this girl, and that worried me.

'That's my problem to deal with; you'll have your own to handle.'

'What do I have to do?'

'You're going to teleport into the basement.'

'You said it was impossible to teleport blind.'

'Yes, it could get you killed if you reappear inside a solid object.'

'You're not selling this to me.'

She placed her phone on the floor. There were fifteen minutes left. I stared at the device and set the countdown as a mental image in my brain.

'The layout is in my head. You'll read my mind and see what it looks like.'

'Don't you mean what it looked like two hundred years ago? All kinds of things will be different now.'

She ran her fingers over mine. 'I was in that room less than a month ago. You'll be safe with what's in my head.'

'A month ago? You were enslaved in this house again?' Sorrow welled up inside me. How was it possible to feel like this for a vampire?

'It doesn't matter. There's not much time left, Cassie. Are you going to do it?' She gripped my hands.

I gazed into her eyes and searched for the memories she focused on. The room came to me in a flash; I was seeing every piece of furniture, every gap, all the nooks and crannies, every shadowed space. There was a table in the far corner of the room and an opening large enough to fit a crouching teenage girl underneath it. That's where I'd land.

I should have looked away then, retreated from her memories, but I tuned into another part of her past, and to the horror she'd endured: rows of kids chained against the wall, and on the end, the terror-filled eyes of Claudia. My mind fled from hers in a jolt; pain seeped into my skull as I gripped her hands.

'All those children were vampires?'

'Yes,' she replied.

'But why?'

'They get made to order. If you're rich or privileged and your tastes run to certain things, then what better than to have a child who'll never age?'

I pulled away from her and wanted to puke. I had to hold on to my guts to stop it from happening.

'And humans do this with the help of other vampires?'

'Yes, they do. Some are in the room below us.'

Anger sped through me like a locomotive. 'Are there any innocents in that basement?'

'No. Not a single one.'

'Good.'

I closed my eyes and picked that spot under the table.

And I hoped for the best.

23 ALICE

His pupils were black, without a spark of light anywhere in them. The room pumped out hot air as if it was going out of fashion, yet the touch of his hand chilled my flesh.

The watch on my wrist said ten minutes left.

I gripped his fingers and expanded my mind, reaching through the darkness and into the abyss of his thoughts. Blackness surrounded me, more absence of light. There was no sound either until the sobbing started.

Hello.

My voice echoed inside my head and his. I moved towards the crying, feet struggling through nothing like they were walking in molasses. The weeping stopped.

Help me.

It was a man's voice as a child. From the shadows, his body unfurled from the foetal position: the leader of this country, ready to unleash nuclear destruction amongst us all. His eyes peered at me. They weren't black now, tears of light glittering on his cheek. The Prime Minister reduced to a whimpering babe. In his hand was a small device with a bright red button in the middle. I assumed it wasn't the actual representation of the nuclear button but something his mind, or mine, had highlighted as the switch to end the world. He glanced at me before placing his thumb over the button, with tears streaming down his face. A silent howl consumed him.

Even after all this time, it still amazes me how feeble the human mind is.

Michael stepped from the gloom behind the man he controlled.

This specimen is weak. How do humans pick someone like this as their leader?

How are you here?

Had he defeated Lucy? Was the Queen of Hell dead? Could these archangels even die?

He pursed his mouth, his tongue slipping over his lips.

There's a little of me in all my subjects; it's much easier to keep them pliable that way, though it places a hell of a strain on me.

I think you may overestimate your strength.

I pointed at his arm as it shimmered in and out of vision. Was he weaker when inside a human? Could I kill him now?

Shock spread across his face, eyes darting from side to side as realisation dropped.

Lucy is here?

The last I saw, she was kicking your arse.

Anything could have been happening in that explosion of light, but he wasn't to know that.

Michael held out his arms. They disappeared, the rest of his body trembling for control. As his grip loosened, life returned to the Prime Minister's eyes. I grasped his hands, his fingers chilled to the bone.

You can break free.

Not with his lack of a spine, he won't.

Michael resumed full form with fingers gripping on to the Prime Minister's shoulders.

I don't need all my concentration to control him.

The light left the Prime Minister's face, skin shrivelling and flesh turning to ice. There were three minutes left on my watch. Michael followed my gaze.

Time is running out. His finger is on the button. Can't you feel it, Alice?

I saw it in the darkness of the PM's eyes, pictured it outside this place and in the physical world, my body fixed on his hand hovering over the nuclear destruct.

Inside the PM's head, I pushed past Michael's manipulation, searching for the heart of this troubled man. I found the genuine parts of him submerged beneath an archangel's anger and frustration. His name was Samuel, his wife Katrina, and their two kids were Harry and Louise: twins.

Look at me, Sam.

My fingers were in his.

Think about Katrina. Imagine your fingers in hers, your arms around your children. Your future is in them; their future is in your hands. You don't want this. If you press that button, what will happen to them?

I turned to face Michael as his voice crawled over my soul.

Do you believe humans care what happens to their children and their children's children? Deep down, they feel nothing for others. They are a selfish and greedy species. They should never have been God's favourite.

Jealousy rippled out of him in waves.

You sound like the jealous one to me.

Michael's hands slithered across Sam's throat. A

mirrored smile crawled from the archangel's face over to the PM. They grinned in unison like evil Cheshire Cats about to devour a mouse.

Ice ran down my spine and it was enough to distract me. The hands were around my throat in an instance, inhuman fingers choking the life from me. My knees bent as I fell to the ground inside Sam's mind.

Why should I be jealous of humans, child?

His grip tightened around my skin.

Every living creature is beneath me, including the Children of the Nephilim. Once I've finished here, I'll find your sister and torture her for centuries. And her pain will be your fault for failing to stop me.

His nails were cutting into my flesh when his words created a spark deep inside me. It started as a murmur somewhere near my heart before roaring through all of me like thunder and lightning. I flexed my mind and threw Michael from me. He skidded along the ground before jumping up.

This is what we have in common, Sister. We should work together, not in opposition.

His words shook me, not for the idea of working with him, but because of the expression he used: Sister. But then I realised he wasn't talking to me, but to Lucy; not here, inside this troubled man's mind, but outside where I assumed they continued to battle.

I returned to the Prime Minister.

Lay down your hand, Sam; look and see what's there.

His illuminated eyes peered past the gloom and what was at his feet.

Pick it up, Sam.

I split my concentration between him and Michael. The archangel stared into the distance, mouthing something I couldn't hear.

Sam picked up the object and lifted it to his face: two small teddy bears joined together. They wore shirts with the names Harry and Louise printed on them. Sam's eyes sparkled as I held my hand out to him. He took it and his skin glowed with warmth. It was the glow of humanity, not destruction.

This isn't over, Alice Arcane. You'll suffer too.

They were Michael's last words before he disappeared.

Sam smiled at me as I vanished from his mind. My vision readjusted into the world, my fingers gripping on to the Prime Minister as he beamed at me.

'Thank you,' he said as he let go and shouted orders to those around him. 'Someone get me the Chinese Premier on the phone. I have bridges to build.'

My arms ached and my head contained a thousand demented jackhammers going wild. I crept past the people trying to bring order from the chaos. I was nearly out of the room when I caught the headline on the giant TV screen.

Something terrible had happened in America.

A cacophony erupted outside the bunker as I landed under the table: screams and gunfire mixed into one. I guessed it was Claudia's distraction. I sprang forward, my mind reaching out like before, forcing every living thing in front of me into the air, and then against the far wall as hard as I could. Bones were smashed, organs shattered, and at least a dozen of Michael's forces slithered to the floor, either dead or dying.

Triggers clicked behind me, my hearing picking up the sounds in the split second before they fired. I threw myself to the ground and rolled beneath a desk; bullets rattled into it as I caught my breath. Blood dripped from my nose, but it was from no gunshot. The walls of my skull vibrated. I ignored the pain. The firing continued as I considered how long they'd wait before coming for me. Then I looked at the timer, counting down inside my head.

Three minutes left.

I had no weapons. Across from me, hanging on the wall, was a large Samurai sword. In the blade's reflection, I saw a dozen guards surrounding the President. What looked like a mobile destruct button was in his hand.

'You can't stop this now, Cassandra.'

Michael's voice came out of the President's mouth. I scanned the room to find who was holding the other destruct button: didn't they need two people pressing buttons simultaneously? I spoke in the hope of a distraction.

'Where's the second person with a finger on the button?'

I ducked my head as bullets whizzed at me. He stood there grinning, squeezed between his security people. There was no way I could teleport or fly between them. My brain hurt too much to use my telekinetic powers again so soon.

The gunfire stopped. They were waiting on the time, confident I had no options remaining.

'Don't be silly, Cassandra; I did away with that stupid security protocol a year ago. Not that we let the public know about it.' He held the portable destruct close to his chest. 'This is all I need to welcome the return of the Creator.'

Time ticked inside my head. Two minutes left.

My fingers trembled as I spoke. 'God wouldn't want this.'

The archangel laughed. 'The first thing the Creator will do on their return will be to thank me for ridding this planet of the Nephilim spawn.'

Blood slid from my eyes and cheeks; hot lava burned through the veins in my legs. I couldn't stand up. My heartbeat was erratic, breathing laboured.

One minute.

I stared at the sword again.

I squeezed my mind and teleported across the room as

tremendous pain shot through my head. I grabbed the blade from the wall and teleported again. The rest of me was numb, but I held on to the weapon, a swirl of colours flashing over my gaze. Bile surged through my guts, desperate to get out of my mouth, but I swallowed to keep it down.

I reappeared above the group of guards, the President crouching in the middle of them. I swung the sword in a circle, one fast motion, and six decapitated heads flew around the room. I dropped to the floor and headless bodies fell with me.

The President's finger was on that button.

Thirty seconds.

There was no strength in me. Blood seeped from my knuckles. The President grinned, and I knew it was Michael looking back at me. I was on the verge of mental and physical collapse. I looked at him one last time before throwing up.

'Farewell, Cassandra Arcane. I'll tell your sister you died in agony.'

As I retched, and with my skull on fire, I reached into every sinew and bone he had, my phantom fingers stretching like long, withered branches on a tree, digging and clawing through each part of him. Then I pulled them apart and scattered him into the four corners of the room. Bones snapped and organs burst. His eyes bulged like balloons overfilled with water till they ruptured into dozens of pieces. His arms and legs flew from his torso, smashing into the walls, blood swirling around the basement.

As he died screaming, my body felt as if it was about to rupture into a thousand parts. The last thing I did was fling my shattered limbs across the ground in one final act of desperation. I caught the mobile destruct button as his fingers split apart, and the device tumbled to the floor.

Five seconds left.

Then I blacked out.

SOMEONE WAS DRAGGING me over the floor as I woke, bits of debris digging into my sides. My skin shivered between temperatures, from freezing cold to burning heat in an instant. It felt like I'd gone ten rounds with the biggest, heaviest boxer in the world.

My eyes flickered into life, my brain emerging from a fog of haze as I remembered what I'd done to the President of the United States of America. I'd murdered him, but it was to save us all.

A hive of activity surrounded me. The police, the FBI, NSA, Homeland Security were everywhere. My ears had shut down, so I couldn't hear what they said, the two FBI agents pulling me away from the chaos. They dragged me from the bunker and into the apocalyptic scene of destruction outside. Bodies were scattered far and wide, throats torn out and heads ripped from shoulders. There was no sign of Claudia.

Someone hauled me through the debris of blood and bone, chains were placed on my hands and feet, then I was thrown into the back of a van. I heard one thing before blacking out again.

'That kid killed the President.'

The screen was full of news of a terrorist attack in the US. Conflicting information filtered out of every media outlet, but they all focused on one fact: somebody had assassinated the President and his cabinet. Cassie had done it; she'd prevented the nuclear onslaught from her end. Now I had to get out of the building and find her.

I staggered past people and nobody stopped me; they were too busy sorting out problems across the UK and the rest of the world. Sam, the man whose mind I'd stumbled inside, appeared agitated as he spoke in Chinese over the phone. There was a mixture of relief and anxiety on the faces of the surrounding staff.

'They think the Chinese might have assassinated the President,' I heard someone whisper as I continued towards the exit. Perhaps we'd only postponed the end of the world. I couldn't focus on that, my weary legs dragging me away while my mind worried about Cassie. I needed to find out what had happened to her.

When I got outside, sirens blared as the police and security forces rushed towards me. Someone shouted orders in my direction as weapons were raised and pointed at my head. It was a muffled concoction of verbal daggers aimed at me, but I picked out a single clear sentence.

'She looks like the other one.'

There was no escaping them. I saw no way out. I pictured the spot where I'd arrived, near the trees in the distance.

Then I vanished.

I reappeared next to the woods and fell to the ground.

As I rolled on to my side, I knew I'd teleported. But that was impossible.

And then the last few minutes made sense.

I'd turned invisible inside that building without knowing it. That's how I'd got past the first group after releasing control of the PM's mind. I must have returned to normal as the security charged towards me. But I couldn't do either of those before.

'You've been able to do these things all along, Alice, just like your sister can.'

Lucy stood before me. I gasped for air, my heart threatening to burst through my ribs.

'It was you who stopped me from using my potential.'

I stuck my fingers into the mud and pushed my body up. It was as if I were wearing lead clothes.

Lucy looked sheepish. 'I put a little block on your abilities, held them back without your knowledge, apart from the telepathy between you and your sister. Your bond was too strong for me to influence that.'

A veil fell from me and revealed all of her deceptions.

'You wanted me to doubt myself, so I'd agree to you coming with me.'

'It seemed the best way to get you to trust me. And it all worked out; well, most of it anyway.'

She plucked a flower from the ground and picked at the petals. A murder of crows jabbered and circled overhead. It sounded like they were laughing at me.

'What did you do?' My teeth rattled against my jaw.

'I imprisoned Michael in the Cage and we stopped a nuclear holocaust. I call that a win.'

'Where's Cassie?' Every part of me seethed with pain, but my strength was returning.

She ripped the flower in half and dropped it to the ground.

'There was one slight problem with our successful outcome. The Americans have locked your sister into the deepest, darkest prison they have. It is a bit of a pickle.'

My fingers trembled as I controlled my rage. 'So you get her and bring her to me.'

'I'd love to do that, Alice, I really would, but those clever Yanks have imprisoned her somewhere I can't access. It would be nice to have both of the Children of the Nephilim with me for when God returns, but I guess one will have to do.'

A volcano of ash seared through my veins. 'You think I'm going with you?'

'You're not in any fit state to stop me, are you? Look, you can barely stand up.'

'Never underestimate the power of anger.'

My mind grabbed at her throat, unearthly fingers pushing tight around her skin. She fell to her knees, hands flailing at her neck as she choked.

'This is impossible.'

'Everything's possible, Lucy; you should know that.'

I lifted her from the ground using my thoughts, the crows shrieking and scattering. I could have crushed every bone in her body if I'd wanted. The power flowing through me was intense, like a drug I needed more of. I released my grip a little to let her speak, but I was in charge.

'You'll burn yourself out, Alice; you're not ready for this. If you use too much now, you'll never be able to use it again.'

She was lying. 'What happens to you if I destroy this human flesh bag you've been wearing for so long? Does your soul disappear into the wind?'

I tightened my invisible grip once more. Lucy struggled for the words as she slowly choked.

'If... you... kill... me... you'll... never... find... your... sister... or your... mother.'

The Queen of Lies was right, but it only fuelled my anger. And my powers were waning like a battery drained in one fell swoop; I couldn't keep it up. But she didn't know that. I released my grip on her throat and dropped her to the grass. A purple bruise was already forming on her neck.

'So what do you propose I do instead of killing you, Queen of Hell?'

A furious buzzing assaulted my brain, my strength dripping out like water from a leaky tap.

'You'll do nothing, Alice Arcane; nothing at all.'

She grinned at me, and then vanished.

My bluff had failed.

I sank into the grass, sitting and staring at the commotion around the mansion. I'd saved the world, we'd saved the world, but still, I'd lost everything.

My sister was imprisoned somewhere even the Devil couldn't get to.

My mother was missing, a hostage to the Lord of Vampires.

And I was a fugitive, a wanted murderer for crimes I hadn't committed.

Yet, I felt more alive and connected to others than ever before.

I stood and took in the air. My fingers tingled with something that wasn't there before. I strode down the hill and from the chaos behind me.

My life hadn't become more complex but more straightforward. I only had one decision to make: to find my family, which I swore to do.

And I never break a promise.

THANK YOU!

Thank you, dear reader for purchasing this book.

If you enjoyed reading about Alice and Cassie Arcane their journey continues in these books:

The Arcane Supernatural Thriller Series
Book one: The Arcane
Book two: The Arcane Identity
Book three: The Arcane Quest
Book four: The Arcane Ultimatum

Many thanks to my wonderful wife for all her support and patience.

My eternal gratitude to Wendy Cross for being the first person to read the Arcane and who gave me essential feedback on the characters and the plot.

Extra special thanks to Karina Gallagher for being a dedicated reader of my work.

The Arcane Identity edited by Alison Jack.

Cover design by James, GoOnWrite.com

ABOUT THE AUTHOR

Andrew French lives amongst faded seaside glamour on the North East coast of England. He likes gin and cats but not together, new music and old movies, curry and ice cream. Slow bike rides and long walks to the pub are his usual exercise, as well as flicking through the pages of good books and the memoirs of bad people.

Find out more at www.andrewsfrench.com

Facebook:

https://www.facebook.com/A-S-French-Author-150145625006018

Twitter:

www.twitter.com/andrewfrench100

Instagram:

www.instagram.com/andrewfrench100

And replies to all his email at mail@andrewsfrench.com

If you have the time, please leave a review at Amazon or Goodreads

Thank you!